CHRISTINE
and her
TEACHEST

by

Robbie Moffat

PALM TREE PUBLISHING

PALM TREE PUBLISHING
Paisley, Scotland Pa1 1TJ

© Robbie Moffat 2010-2019

First published in digital form in JULY 2014
First published in paperback JANUARY 2019

Typeset: Verdana 10pt

ISBN-10: 0 907282 34 2
ISBN-13: 9780907282341

PREFACE by Louis

The year was 1986. I met Christine at a party. She took me home to her run down little rented flat on the other side of the town moor and fucked me. I fell in love.

I had always fancied myself as a writer, but from the moment I started hanging out with Christine, I discovered she was a genius of invention and imagination. Inside Christine's head was a whole world that could relate to most things in the solar system. To top it, she wrote a lot of her imaginings down, but as a truly creative person, she found it hard to be commercial. She kept everything in a tea chest.

I was just a pretentious hack. I found that to put everything down on paper was one of the most boring things in the entire universe. Anyone who's familiar with Limbo, the first ring you pass through on the way to Hell, will understand what it's like to be an uninspired storyteller. I kept most things in my head and wrote very little.

This story is thus two stories. The first is the story Christine wanted to write and put in her tea chest, and the other is the story I, Louis wanted to write about Christine who dragged me through Limbo and across the river Styx.

As our love affair began its roller coaster ride across the continents of the world, our war of words began.

MY STORY

I am in a prison, a cell where no light enters, where no sound exits. I am alone, I hear nothing, and see only the figments of my own imagination. I have a past, but what use is a past when there seems to be no future. It is dark in here, yet here is where I must remain until my time is served.

My crime? It is a secret that wells up within me until I cannot speak. And then ... who will listen? These walls are silent, each brick a day of time. My mind caught up in a heady race against my body, my weak limbed corpse a sallow frame of neglect and unkemptness. My thoughts walk pastures, but my being is immersed in sickness and night.

I have been unbending in my outlook. I have been unrepentant of my deeds. I am cold and hungry, but I know I will not die.

Christine put down her pen. You see, Christine didn't have to tell me that Britain is no place to be a nobody. If you allow yourself to condone all the infamies and atrocities perpetrated by any Antichrist (usually the Prime Minister) then let us part ways now. You can be no friend of ours if you think that unemployment is a nasty disease. When you reach Christine's level of creativity, then, you have to give up real work. Unemployment has time on its side, and the re-assurance that you don't work for someone else. But that sort of logic kind of defeats the whole purpose of being a storyteller.

"Do you see what it means? If you don't, then you must know a better way to make a living than trying to tell people something they already know."

That's what Christine told me.

I suppose Christine believes that she knows lots of things that other people don't know. We all have secrets, and I suppose that's what it's all about ... keeping quiet when you have to, and opening your gob when it's an advantage. One famous poet I know uses the word gob a lot when he's talking about mouthing-off. Like him, Christine often gets hung up on words ... that's part of her storyteller's art, but Christine's doesn't off-load all her views on art in her work. That would be a big blunder ... she'd be giving all her secrets away. She wants to keep her best secrets for her best seller.

So what's she told me, and what am I going to tell you? I've got this picture of how Christine should be, and she's got this idea of how the world should be, and how it is, and what it really was, and maybe it'd be best if we just got on with it.

THE LITTLE GIRL

The sun flirts through the trees to catch the ribbon in the hair of Caroline. The ducks squabble for the pieces of bread she breaks between her fingers and cast upon the water. She is a beautiful girl; her long blonde locks falling to her waist. Her dress is blue polka-dotted, and her legs are long and slender. An old man on a park bench eyes her with slavered mouth. He calls to her, but she does not hear. Her ears are with the ducks and trees, and the water lapped by the breeze on to her sandals. Her world is free and innocent of darkness and worry. She sees the old man drooling on himself, his hands fumbling in his pockets. He is looking for his gold watch or a bag of crumbs to feed the pigeons gathered at his feet. Or else, he feels the cold of autumn on his back, and is counting pennies for a cup of tea.

Christine stopped for a moment and thought that what she had just written was the sort of story her agent would send back to her marked UNMARKETABLE. She could not understand whether her agent thought the story rubbish or the publishing world unready.

"Fuck it!" Christine despaired.

Maybe I should let her explain some more. We were sitting in her office having Nicaraguan coffee.

"You see, I began writing when I was seventeen, sort of a late starter in the business compared with some of these Oxbridge types. Looking back on it though, seventeen seems pitifully young for anyone to commit himself or herself to a profession. I suppose things could have been worse. My brother Harry got engaged when he was sixteen because he thought he was getting old. I mean, that's real commitment. Yet again, he called the whole thing off when he was seventeen because his fiancé didn't want to go around the world. It was crazy really; they didn't have money to go anywhere. It was the idea, the principle. Harry just couldn't stand the notion of being with some one who didn't want to go anywhere. He felt tied down ... understandable at any age, never mind seventeen."

She paused.

"At thirty, I feel the same way. And heh ... if I'm not sincere, let the heavy axe fall."

Christine scratched her nose, and continued with her work.

THE OLD MAN

The old man stumbles home to his abode. The cats crowd around him for their milk. Nine ... ten ... eleven ... one is missing - the shy old Tom he took in the year before. Next door he hears the neighbours arguing over sex. He's seen the comings and goings of the faithless wife's lovers ... an endless stream of young men ... while the husband's been on the oil rigs.

The old man, grey with stubble, his scalp beneath his flat-cap, blotched and bald, shouts "Be quiet, you bastards!" then passes to the kitchen, and the kettle, and the stove, to make some tea.

In Christine's mind, love conquers all. Many have been her lonely nights in the blue walled rooms of far-flung hostelries.

"These were the moments when my writing filled the gaping void that a storyteller must descend into to find the secrets of her art. Sometimes other lonely individuals would inhabit the void and we'd drink tea or share some tobacco. There are many cherished moments still vivid in my mind, and many other times less ready to be brooked that I have jotted in a notebook which now lies at the bottom of a tea chest."

You see, Christine's tea chest is her cauldron, her manuscripts her brew. Just like Gwion Bach.

GWION BACH

When Gwion Bach drank the three drops of wisdom potion meant for the son of Ceridwen, to escape the wrath of the angered mother, he transformed himself into a hare. Ceridwen pursued him as a greyhound. Gwion left into a river and became a fish. Ceridwen chased him as an otter. Gwion became a bird, Ceridwen a hawk. Gwion turned into a grain of wheat, and dropped among the grains on a threshing floor. Ceridwen became a black hen and swallowed him up. Nine months after, Ceridwen bore Gwion as an infant. She would have killed him, but he was so beautiful, she wrapped him in a leather bag and cast him into the sea. The infant Gwion drifted to shore where he was found and called Taliesin, Beautiful Brow. Taliesin grew up to become the most renowned poet of the Cymry, the Welsh peoples of pre-Saxon Britain.

Christine's cauldron is her tea chest.

Anyone daring enough to steal three drops of wisdom from her storyteller's vessel might come away with a brew strong enough to transform any individual into a poet. The magic of words work in mysterious ways ... the fantasy of fiction has its own fascination.

THE NEIGHBOURS

The neighbours are un-reconciled. The husband puts on his coat, slaps his wife across the face, and slams the door.

She watches as he rushes down the street to the house of his divorcee mistress, but he turns the corner. She lives many districts away in another part of town.

She turns and puts the kettle on for tea. It is five o'clock, and soon her lover will be home for dinner. She counts the flying ducks on the wall above the music centre. One is missing ... it lies on the turntable in four broken pieces ... the beak, the tail, the two wings. The shot bird recalls ten years of marriage, and she cries as the doorbell sounds.

It is the milkman collecting the monthly dues on his deliveries. Wiping her tears, unfussy she pays him, lets him quickly go with a whistle on his lips to knock upon the door of the old man next door.

Christine, aware of the emptiness in her own life, saw it in other' lives too. "You know, some people see this whole world as one great big pond." She pulled a poem out of her tea chest, and handed it to me.

ALL MY FRIENDS ARE LITTLE FROGGIES
WHO LIVE IN A POND,
AND EACH LITTLE FROGGY
LIVES IN A WORLD OF HIS OWN.
EACH HAS A GREEN LEAF
WHICH HE CALLS AS A HOME
IN A POND WHERE EACH FROGGY
IS BORED TO THE BONE.

Christine sighed with boredom. Her friend Mavis was like that.

MAVIS

"She never goes diving. She can swim ... but she's definitely better at hopping. When she goes out it's to a nearby leaf. She doesn't swim; she just hops from leaf to leaf. What happens under the pond ... well, that's a mystery to Mavis. She's never found out what happens beneath her, and never will. It's of little concern to her; all that matters to Mavis is herself and her friends. She doesn't really care much about the pond, apart from the part she's on. Yet really, she doesn't know that part either because she doesn't swim. Her knowledge of her part of the pond is pretty thin. If she decided to dive deep and leave the security of the leaves behind, she wouldn't be risking more than a few watery hopes."

When all is said and done, there are countless froggies like Mavis in the pond. There are many parts we've heard of, but more we know nothing of at all. I know Christine would like to see the froggies dive a little deeper, so that the pond might become more than just a green patch, but we all know that's Cinderella thinking. We all know that the world is really ruled by toads.

Christine picked up her pen.

THE MILKMAN

The milkman sees everything. He starts his rounds at four a.m. he knows an easy lay when he does his rounds. Many women are tired of husbands, but more are lonely and need the comfort of a few warm words.

The milkman sees, but he never tells what he sees, for his gossip is the confidence of his customers. He is always first in bed, and first away to attend to his business. He prefers the summer months to the darkness of winter. He receives little joy from burning his hands on frozen double creams. There is little homely comfort on snow-thick mornings, few welcome comings and goings from friendly housewives.

The milkman prefers the spring and summer, when like the early bird, he is first to enjoy the fruit of life new-sprung. His preference is for beauty and youth, and not for old men with cats to feed and no money with which to pay a six-month milk bill.

The milkman sees it all, the comings and the goings, as he gives up on the old man, and passes by the Widow-with-a-Family's door one up from the old man.

Christine pulled another secret from her tea chest. I let her put on her spectacles, for it was growing dark outside. "Yes, yes..." she said, "I remember this." She paused for a moment. I lit a cigarette with some hashish inside, took a draw and then passed it to her. "Can I read you this?" she asked. I nodded, and let my gaze drift across her walls of Bob Dylan and Eric Clapton posters.

"GO ON, MALCOLM. I LOVE YOU!" she said.

"I WILL! I WILL!" Malc cried.

"COME ON, SON." the copper said quietly.

"BOG OFF, YOU SILLY CUNTS!"

"THAT'S IT, MALCOLM. SHOW THE BUGGERS!" Stef encouraged.

"ANYMORE OF THAT, MY GIRL" the inspector warned "AN' WE'LL 'AVE U IN A CELL FOR THE NIGHT."

"HE'S GOING TO DO IT, SIR!" a young bobby shouted.

"WE'LL 'AVE 'IM FOR THIS!" the inspector screamed.

"GO ON, MALCOLM! YOU KNOW I LOVE YOU!"

"SERGEANT! LOCK 'ER UP! INCITEMENT TO RIOT!" the inspector specified.

"LEAVE HER ALONE, PINHEADS!!" Malcolm roared.

"THEY CAN'T TOUCH ME, MALCOLM."

"COME ON, U IDIOTS" the inspector yelled "'AND CUFF HER!"

"I'LL DO IT! I'LL DO IT!" Malcolm threatened with a lift of his gigantic arm.

"FUCKIN' ELL" the inspector gasped putting his hands to his ears.

Malcolm no longer in control of his rage smashed the arm of the JCB digger through the front of W.H.Smith's plate glass window.

"THAT'LL TEACH THE BASTARDS. THEY SHOULDN'T HAVE BLOODY FIRED MY GIRLFRIEND. UP THE LOT OF YOU!"

He wheeled the digger around and went smashing into the record and tape counter, then headed for the typewriters. A dozen pinheads swarmed all over the cab of the digger, got him by the neck, and hauled him out. They beat hell out of him, but Malcolm knew he had won. He had bought his own bit of social justice. He was an anarchist who knew what the people thought. He knew he'd be a hero, but better than that, he knew he was really in love.

Christine stopped reading. She threw the story back into the tea chest and said "Un-publishable." I nodded ... the hashish had gone straight to my head. "Can't use words like fuck and cunt and hope to be successful." I agreed.

I turned my tape-recorder off and rolled another spliff. She excused herself for a few minutes and went to the loo. Lying on her desk was part six of her latest novel.

MUM

It was a big family ... nine kids - Ed, Ted, and Fred; April, May, and June; Fran and Fanny the twins; and Chris who was born at Christmas.

Dad had died from cancer six years before. His portrait stood on the mantle-piece. Mum also had a miniature of dad by her bedside. It was a fact that Mum had never kissed a man since she had touched Dad's cold lips at the wake. She was a good religious woman who took her chapel visits as a duty. Motherhood had brought her closer to Mother Mary. A life of chastity and godliness lay before her.

June, her most innocent daughter, was being prepared for the convent of St.Mary, a sisterhood of the utmost piety and dedication to God. Sometimes Mum would give the old man next door some food-scraps for his cats. She was a tender-hearted woman. More than once, she had sheltered a battered wife from the crimes of an irate husband. It was her calling to be kind, supportive, and motherly.

But if there was one thing that upset Mum, it was the rowdy youngsters who occupied the house across the street. She had heard that they didn't pay any rent, and that they had resisted every kind of effort to coax them to move.

Christine returned from the loo and caught me reading her work. She didn't seem to mind. She explained that little of her writing was private any more. Taking a long draw on the spliff, she began to explain.

"Usually when I tell a story."

Just at that moment, the Victorian doorbell tinkled.

"Excuse me a moment."

She left me holding the hashish. Bob Dylan's *42nd Street* face stared down at me, and as I turned away, I caught sight of Jimi Hendrix's *Band of Gypsies* sticking out from behind a wardrobe. I wondered how it was she had managed to hold on to such ancient posters. It convinced me that somewhere in her flat she had a complete set of Beatles records stashed away.

"Hello, Alice." Christine's voice carried up the stairs. The sound of footsteps followed. "Cup of tea...?" I heard Christine mutter. "Put the kettle on will you, Alice..." There was a short pause, and then Christine rejoined me in her office.

"Sorry about that ... Alice ... a good friend of mine. Comes over to do my typing for me. Two pounds an hour? At one point, well that was before she started, she wanted to do it for nothing.

"Talking to yourself again, Chris?" Alice shouted from the kitchen.

"Reading a story, Alice."

THE OLD TODA

There are many old men in the world who spend their last days upon a hillside watching the sun rise and set, yet there are few who could claim to be last of their tribe.

One such man, toothless, weathered, and crippled by the enormity of the years he has survived, is still well enough to see and hear the visitors who come to him from the city below. In his boyhood, the new city was a sheltered area nestling between forested slopes. Those were days when the lake to the north of the city was twice its present size. The streams that raged in the rainy season did not disappear underground to re-emerge with the waste of two hundred thousand city dwellers. Days of dear and wild fowl, camp fires and mud huts built into the hillside. Days far too long to remember, days long gone.

Now only one man can tell of those days, for in his tribe no-one thought to write things down that seemed so normal then. All knowledge had been passed down from father to son, or learned through experience with life and the spirits that must have existed then, or at least through the songs of the old wives and the wisdom of the blind old men. No one knew of writing, and only a few had time to carve figures on pieces of bark wood with wood ash, or sculpt shapes on boulders of soft stone.

So what had become of the tribe?

Only the old man on the hillside knew. Visitors came every day to see him, but few asked any questions, as they could not speak his native tongue. Most left a few small coins in the bowl in front of him, but they left with their questions unanswered and the mystery unsolved.

Yet, the old man did not seem to care. He was happy to keep his memories to himself. The tribe was gone, and talking would not bring it back. The days of wild deer and a habitat of forested hillside lived on only in the old man's mind as he watched the sun rise and set over the city.

"Alice" Christine said as she finished reading the story of the Old Toda which she had scooped up out of her tea-chest "I might have this one typed out." Alice was next door typing away. She stopped.

"What about the manifesto I'm doing?"

"I've got some doubts about it."

"To be honest, I can't understand a word of it, Chris."

"Is it my handwriting, Alice?"

"No. You know I've got that down now."

Christine turned to me. "The Manifesto's heavy stuff. Luckily I latched on to Matthew Arnold's *Sweetness and Light* for some structure to build around."

I was unimpressed. "What are you going to do with the manifesto."

"Send it to the bloody Arts Council. I can't think of anyone else who should read it more. Of course they won't understand it. They don't understand anything in Piccadilly."

"Do you want me to leave off typing the Manifesto, Chris?" Alice asked from the next room.

"Hell no! The Old Toda story can wait. Finish it. I'll post it this afternoon and be damned."

I looked at Christine and suddenly felt that maybe, if everything went just right, I could fall in love with her.

TOM

The old man's Tom was always stoned. The Youngsters across the street fed him hashish. It made them feel that they were living the life of a comic strip, and besides, they liked the randy old cat, it knew how to pounce on people they didn't like.

The Youngsters are always nervous. They live under the constant threat of a police siege. This is not idle fantasy. The Youngsters have many items in their house that are not legal. It is as silly to name them as it is for the police to seize them. The Youngsters are only damaging themselves though they believe that they are heading like Mum, towards the light and the truth. As a result, they find little time to wash the dishes or cook anything more enterprising than baked beans. They do however forbid anyone to bring meat into the house unless it is Christmas. This means that the old man's Tom has to eat out a lot, but as there is an Indian restaurant down the street, this is no problem.

The owner of the Indian restaurant is the Youngsters' landlord, and it is true that they haven't paid the rent for fifteen months.

Christine is a fast worker, she managed to rattle off a chapter while Alice and I sat and had a cup of tea. There wasn't much conversation. Just as well, Alice is a funny old bird. You'd think she was about fifty-five. My god, I've never seen such an assembly of parts make up a person. I mean, she's human, but when you look at her sometimes, you think, "Naw, no-one could be that unlucky." You know what I mean. Well, not all of us can be perfect, but Alice ... man, her eyes pop right out of her head. Gosh, whatever you do, don't give her a biscuit; you'll end up with crumbs everywhere. I've never seen anyone consume so much, remain so skinny, and be so stingy. Chris has to hide the fast foods when Alice shows up or it's gone. If you offer Alice anything, she never says no. I'd offer her my body, but she might not give it back.

I mean, she's got a nice smile when there's no crumbs hanging off her chin, but the rest of her, well, I think I'll stick with Christine. You see, Alice is a bit lost. Sure, she's got the Church and she goes and hides out at these Christian retreats for weeks on end, but it's hardly what I'd call living. Of course, her great artistic interest is music, and in a way she' quite knowledgeable. It is just such a great pity that she's so boring. I mean, if she doesn't get into the conversation she falls asleep. Come to think of it, she sends me to sleep.

"Chris ... I've got to go now. I've got a piano lesson in an hour."

Christine looked up. "Okay, Alice."

"Will you be in tomorrow?"

"Eh ... in the morning. If I go out I'll leave the back door open for you, Alice."

"I like working on that interview you did with the Californian poet. She sounds an amazing woman. Seven children, and then going to Art College!"

Christine swiveled on her chair "Mary took me under her wing when I lived in the Bay Area. She introduced me to the West

Coast poetry school. I spent..."

"I'd love to hear it Chris, but I've got to go. Maybe I'll see you tomorrow?"

"Alright, Alice."

"I'll do some work on the Seven Sisters tomorrow."

"Okay."

"Got to go."

I was sitting thinking "Go on, go." Watching her trying to leave was like having a tooth pulled. It was sheer agony.

"You don't mind, Chris."

"O for God's sake, Alice."

"Alright. See you tomorrow."

She finally went.

No sooner was she gone than Chris and I were back in bed having a good old fuck.

HARI AND PADDY

Hari Singh, the owner of the Indian restaurant, is a very nice man. He has paid for seven of his British Subject cousins and nephews to come to wonderful Margaret Thatcher England from the Punjab, and he has managed to arrange fine Indian wives for them all. However, Hari can do nothing with his own sons. They are wayward and thoroughly British. The last time he had seen his youngest boy Ram, his hair had been dyed green. Hari, inflamed by his son's flouting, felt that he was now unfit to have the holy name of Ram. He renamed him Oscar.

"Now that be a fine Irish name at that." Patrick O'Toole consoled him.

"O Paddy ... you do not know the shame

I suffer by my children. If it were India" he said with a sad rolling of his eyes *"my neighbours would think that he had turned Hindu. I would not be allowed into the Golden Temple. You see what happens when a man gives up his British Subject status and decides to become a British Citizen. It is not very nice."*

"Now shoush there, Hari, me ol' china. It's only green dye. I've seen worse colouring on county Cork sheep."

Poor Hari.

Paddy O'Toole was his favourite customer. They had struck up a friendship over many years. They didn't come to England on the same boat but the came about the same time. Paddy had had his fair share of up so downs since he'd left the Mother country across the water. Paddy gave Hari a fellow outsider's view of the English, and naturally, it was not always a glowing report. In fact, Paddy O'Toole was darn right scathing when he got the brogue marching across his tongue. In return, Hari sold Paddy drinks outside the regular licensing laws. It was a good friendship.

"The pubs are open all day in Ireland." Patrick was in the habit of boasting. *"*

"Acha ... in India our chai-shops are open twenty-five hours a day."

"Don't you think the English drink too much tea, me pal?"

"I do not know" Hari said *"but I think the Irish make too much of the English."*

Just then, the postman arrived with a parcel for Hari's son Ram. It was from India, and Hari signed for it.

"A gift from the family of the girl I want him to marry."

"Smells very strange." said the postman.

Christine and I were in bed. I was as randy as hell, but Christine was holding me back.

"One story I remember" she said without dipping into her tea-chest "... part of growing up you might say ... was my first visit to the Family Planning Clinic. I was sixteen, no, seventeen, and me mum had told me that if I was going to do it, then I might as well do it properly. But when it came to the reality, she was aghast. Then she lightened up and seemed pleased that I was having healthy sexual relations with a steady boyfriend.

But actually, there was no one I really fancied, though I did do it now and then with Bill Full. I decided that I wanted a cap.

"You have a steady boyfriend, Miss Christine?" the nurse asked me. I assumed she was a nurse. She was more obsessed than mum about the steady boyfriend bit.

"O yes, of course!" I lied.

"And what does he do?" she asked.

"He uses Durex" I replied.

God, I was so naive then. I went completely beetroot when I realised what she actually meant.

I've never written this story down" Christine told me while stroking my nipple "I've always kept it as one of my spontaneous party pieces. When I want to display innocence in sexual matters, out it comes. But really, it is also an attempt to shock, which it never does. Perhaps it is part of the schoolgirl that lingers on in me, the lack of sexual experience that I'm sure I'd be curious to possess given the right circumstances. Yet it is the waiting for the circumstances rather than a following up of desire that keeps me from being worldlier. This of course is different from being womanly; there are so many sides to our image of woman that sex, major though it is, is a minor part of the whole woman. Sex is a fulfillment, and it does not lead to any significant achievement for a woman, except children. Enjoyment and gratification is one thing, love and happiness are another. The two become one with the right person."

Christine kissed me so passionately; I did not need to give a verbal response. And anyway, what the hell could I have said after all that without committing myself feet first. I was like a big flounder that had been let off the hook.

DANNY

Like the milkman, Danny the Postman knew everybody's business. He could tell whether a letter contained a postal order or a giro cheque, a love note or a 'dear john', pools win or a final demand. American letters usually contained money, Indian letters drugs.

But the postman, himself a young man, turned a blind feel to such hedonistic excesses. The only thing he confiscated was the sado-maso porn mags from Denmark that were sent on subscription to Thrasher Jones who rented the flat above the chip-shop. Anything else, he let it pass through his fingers, though at certain quiet moments he found time to open the odd letter for personal amusement. He knew all about the landlord of the Junk and Crusher and the long platonic declarations that his gay lover sent to him by first post every Tuesday morning. Of course, Danny could never tell anyone else. It would be the end. Six months in jail for opening mail. But Danny knew that the landlord of the Junk and Crusher knew that Danny knew what was being communicated in the letters. There was an uncommunicative silence between Danny and the landlord when he popped in for a quick pint. A suggestive quiver of an eyelid, the odd smirk, the occasional limp wrist, the frequent squirm of buttocks, and the ever present sharp bitchy wit ... were all dead give-aways. The closet case who couldn't liberate himself.

However, Danny the Postman was more interested in re-licking the stamps of Daisy the Barmaid who had taken him home once after a Saturday night lock-in.

I moved in with Christine after a week in bed. I'd just come back from South Africa where people were killing each other on a larger scale than in Northern Ireland. I had been staying with a veggie friend, and had been off the plane from Joburg four days when I was introduced to Christine the Writer. Things just blew along faster than

Hurricane Charley.

Christine got up about eleven, went downstairs, and brought the mail back up to the bedroom.

"Got a letter from Barclays..."

"Should get out of them right now. They're all for inequality."

"I don't have to open it" she said. "It must have been the new writing desk I bought for myself last week."

"I think the people in this country don't really care about anything else but themselves" I said.

"I was sick of using a red Formica table to perch my papers on." She was in her own world. "And anyway, I couldn't get my tea-chest under it." She threw the Barclay's letter into the bin.

I was reading the *Life of Balzac*. Yeah, I thought, that's how writers end up bankrupt, they throw their overdraft statements into the bin without reading them. No, it could never happen to me, that's what they all tell themselves.

Chrissy must have been reading my thoughts. "They don't have debtors prisons anymore" she said flippantly before she picked the statement back out of the bin.

"This Frenchman owed millions," I said pointing to my book.

"You don't have to tell me about Balzac. The poor bugger had to write himself to death to pay for his bourgeoisie living style."

"It was the women that got him."

"Well that won't be my downfall, honey."

I suddenly saw Christine in a new light "God, you're vain," I said.

"Not as vain as Sir Walter Scott. He published so many of his own books that he couldn't keep up with the printer's costs. Or something like that. I never seem to get these things right. One thing though, Balzac and Scott were prolific novelists because they were up to their eyeballs in debt."

Christine opened the letter from Barclays. "Well" she said, "I've got the debt, but no publisher. I've five novels and a book of short stories in my tea chest. Maybe if I cultivate my debts, my publishing chances will grow."

I liked the desk though. She'd bought a box of paper clips to give that authentic looking touch. She had two staple guns and generally used plastic slide binders. The paper clips were just for show.

"It is silly" she said, "I suppose I didn't have to buy the desk. I never write at desks anyway. I hate hard seats. I love to lie in bed with the pillows under my head and dream. That's much better than pulling a ballpoint pen across a blank piece of paper. I'm tempted ... now that I've got Alice ... to use a tape recorder instead of a pen. I know loads of writers who never write a thing."

Suddenly Christine was rummaging under the bed. She produced a tape recorder and plugged it into the wall socket across the room.

"Damn! The lead on the recorder won't reach as far as the bed. It's totally useless. O hell, it's no good anyway. I'm no poet.

You have to be a poet to compose verbally, otherwise, you end up being a hack."

By this time it was impossible to relax. If there is one thing about Christine that is really unsettling, then, it's her restlessness. She never stops talking.

"I wrote a poem about hacks once. I wrote it for the chairman of the Arts Council Literature Panel. I sent a copy to the National Poetry Secretariat, anonymous of course. No address, so no reply, so I never did find out what they thought of it. I've got a copy of it in my tea chest, and another four hundred copies under the bed. Take a look."

I struggled to the edge of the bed and looked under.

"That's where I keep all my publications," she said.

She pulled out a copy of MacHack and handed it to me. I read a few lines.

MACHACK

I've heard that goddess Dullness has been set above the poets that abound the lists of Art Council scribblers and that each to get his pennies from the State must first of all agree not to write the truth or say a word against the leaders of the country, and that all their verse must be published by the friends of friends of friends of government ministers of the Tory faction, which of course so they say are the only ones who can afford to pay the scandalous prices for the briefest lines of piss-pot bumf that finds its way on to the shelves of all

*the public libraries in the country where its
ignored as it hasn't got anything to do with
people who use the public libraries up and
down the country.*

The thing went on and on. It wasn't my
cup of tea as far as poetry goes. I think I'd
rather read about daffodils, and I told
Christine that. She didn't seem in the least
bit bothered.

"My exposed work goes under the bed,
my unpublished in the tea-chest. I'd show
you more of the stuff under the bed, but
being underground material, I quite like the
idea that it is obscure and irrelevant.
Irrelevant to publishers, that is. They're not
interested in subversive stuff. They want
good British trash."

She picked up a ballpoint and began
writing.

DAISY

*Daisy was only nineteen, and a second
year English literature student at the
University. Her parents refused to pay their
parental contribution to her grant
allowance. An American friend told her to
sue her parents, but it is just not the British
way. As a result, while the rest of Daisy's
fellow students spent money on clothes and
discos, Daisy had to go out and make
money to pay the rent and bring home the
baked beans. The responsibility made her
far too level headed ... not such a bad thing
for a student ... but having to work all
hours affected her studies. While the smart-
wallies and winnies wrote their weekly*

course essays and submitted them type perfect to their approving tutors, Daisy struggled between lectures and two jobs to research and write an essay once a month. Occasionally she had time for sex with blokes like Danny the Postman, but they were one-offs. In her three-day job at the Penny Farthing craft shop, she spent much of her time fending off the advances of Slick Vic, the owner, who had employed her for her good looks. After a little while, Daisy began to see her job at Penny Farthing as a kind of prostitution worth one pound twenty pence an hour that made her feel pretty cheap.

It was such a shame. Daisy was a pretty girl of high intelligence, who for the sake of a few hundred pounds a term was descending into a slimy-hand world. Of all the people she had met since coming to town, she loved her tutor most. He loved her too, but for professional reasons he could only comfort her intellectually. You see - Len was married. Daisy didn't mind some night tutoring, but he never suggested it.

The fool!

Christine and I were in the bath. She was spouting on.

"Some stories get written on trains, others on planes, but very few in the bath."

I grabbed the sponge and stuffed it in her ... mouth.

A great fight ensued. We completely flooded the bathroom. We were just about to get it on when the doorbell rang.

Christine jumped out the bath and ran naked downstairs to the door. I lay in the bath and wondered whom this Len the Tutor she'd written about really was.

LEN

Len the Tutor was a man of great academic potential. He was the youngest senior lecturer in the whole University. This meant two things. One - he was the least respected. Two - he earned a lot of money for his age.

But Len had overheads. His books for research cost him a thousand pounds a year. His wine bill was even more horrendous. It seemed that there was always some poor nationally recognised poet living on at his house after coming from the ends of the country to give a free recital that no one attended. Anthony ... Adrian … Alistair ... Andrew ... it seemed they'd all spent several weeks at Len's place under the pretext that they were in the process of completing their latest volume. To them, Len was a patron of the literary arts.

As an academic, Len judged their 'volumes' to be very slim. If he were a man given to complaint, he could boast that each poem in these slim volumes had cost him, on average, five bottles of wine. Yet, as a patron of the arts, he constantly muttered to himself "Wine is the blood of gods, and the nectar of poets." Somewhere at the back of his mind ran the words "To feed a poet is polite, but to give him wine is to make him immortal."

Well, that may be so, but he hardly enjoyed the intensity of his poet 'friends'. Len's real friends were his students, and despite seeming to be rather peculiar to the younger generation that surrounded him, they liked him. For there was one strange thing about Len's personality that made more than just a few students wary of his sexual nature ... he had a pet monkey. A potty aristocrat called Dom Pedro who had read Len's memorable book about Rochester, the seventeenth century fornicator, had given it to him. Len had sent a thank you letter.

> Dear Dom,
> In humble appreciation of your fine gift, I find it inconceivable that I can give Wilmot the home he would otherwise enjoy in his native land. I therefore beg that you take the poor homesick creature back to the upper reaches of the Amazon, as I am afraid that the cold northern winds of England might turn him blue. I love him very much but I cannot bring myself to accept such a generous gift.

Len had held on to Wilmot until he had received a reply. But none came. Dom Pedro had gone back to Brazil. Caught holding the monkey, Len had to adopt Wilmot as one of his own.

I was still in the bath. I could hear

voices downstairs. I could just about make out what they were saying.

"Can I borrow a couple o' quid, Chris?"

"Sure, Jan. Let me just find my purse."

"Can I sell you some' it. I'm short a' cash. The baby's not eaten today. I need to buy milk an' things. I've got a hairdryer,"

"Ah..."

"It's a good ane. Three quid, like?"

"Okay, Jan."

PAUSE.

"We've been disconnected, Chris. Can I use your phone?"

"Go ahead. Local is it?"

"Yeah."

I could hear a ten-figure number being dialed.

"Hello. Dave. I'll be over in a friend's car in an hour. Bye." That's all she said then hung up. I could hear Christine moving about.

"Here's your money, Jan."

"Thanks, Chris. I'll bring the hairdryer around later. You don't want to buy me telephone receiver? I need to pay some bills as well."

"How much, Jan?"

"I need fifteen quid, Chris."

"Oh shit ... I can't afford that."

"Eight pounds?"

"Okay, Jan. I don't know what I'm going to do with it."

Eventually whoever it was left. Christine came back upstairs and pulled out the plug.

"That was Jan. She used to come around and see me a lot. Usually it was for a cup of tea or coffee. Then it changed. She started coming to ask me favours."

"Throw us a towel," I said.

"Do you know I've got three receivers now. Really I only need one. You know how small this place is."

"Who did you say that was?" I asked as I stood dripping on the bath mat.

"Jan Jones. She's pretty far down the heroin road. I worry about her kid. There's another couple I know ... Den and June who lost their baby last year. Story goes that it was a cot death. The little thing was only two months old. Den and June have been addicts for years. Den got convicted again two months ago; I read it in the paper."

"What can be done? People are people; it's their lives. But where does it cross into mine. Jan wanted to use the phone. Sure, I let her. She called her pusher Dave, fixed a deal. She looked like death. She was sweating and cold. Just before she left she said "I nicked a pair of trousers from Bainbridge's today. I was desperate. I just walked out with them. I took them back half and hour later and asked for a refund as I didn't like them. The woman gave me the money. It was the same woman I'd done it with the last time."

What she was saying was something you'd hear in the courts everyday. What can I say? I don't know. I think I'm going to put this story at the very bottom of my tea chest."

WILMOT

Wilmot, Len's pet monkey, had never been to Brazil. He had been bought in Harrods toy store. He had made a trip to Kenya, and had once spent an entire month on a beach in Sri Lanka. He was very well travelled. He never got homesick. He was a bit like Paddington Bear, but instead of coming from darkest Peru, Wilmot had grown up in Chelsea. He had once been the best friend of Amanda, the daughter of a high-ranking Whitehall civil servant called Hincklebottom. The said Hincklebottom had been promoted to the Diplomatic Corp after an indistinguishable career in the Foreign Office. It was John Hincklebottom's unexpected rise to diplomatic status that had enabled Amanda and Wilmot to travel everywhere.

Amanda and Wilmot had been very close, but suddenly one day, Amanda grew up and ran away from home with a boy from Brixton. Poor Wilmot! He was left behind, and sadly with out the warm comfort of Amanda's love, he was neglected. Finally, when Amanda failed to return, he was thrown out of the Hincklebottom home.

Poor Wilmot! He was picked up by a dustman, and after passing through many homes and owners, he ended up in a bric-a-brac shop. By sheer chance, Dom Pedro, his wife expecting a child, purchased him for fifty pence. The sad expression on Wilmot's face had caught the heart of the browsing Brazilian, and when he got Wilmot home, he decided that the creature was too delicate to give to any child as a toy. Out of harms way he placed Wilmot on a shelf.

"Si solo teneo dos mas" he would say in Portuguese, not Spanish, every time he saw Wilmot sitting lonely on the shelf. But he couldn't find two more monkeys like Wilmot. Then one evening, barely a week before he was due to return to Brazil with his spouse and offspring, he read an article in The Times.

ROCHESTER, THE PERVERTED MONKEY LOVER

As an academic book, Len Hand's latest effort Rochester the Perverted Monkey Lover is not everything it seems. On the one hand it is a serious investigation of Rochester the literary genius whose debauched life in Charles the Second's court eventually brought him to an early end. His high-powered sexual nature, his love of other high-powered people's wives, and his overwhelming desires to undo the men as well as the corsets of all the court ladies, led to his downfall. His love of monkeys, and his acute attraction to one in particular, is also attributed to his early death at the age of thirty-three. A man of undeniable literary qualities, his plays and poetry were, and perhaps still are, too blue for public taste.

As a note, we might add that Mr.Hand seems to share Rochester's love of monkeys. When we interviewed him this week, he said he would not turn down a free monkey if someone had one to spare.

*All in all, his book will appeal to those who
wish to know more about the bedroom
indiscretions of the Merry Monarch's nobles.
Rochester the Perverted Monkey Lover is
not for the purist.*

*After reading the review, Dom Pedro
knew exactly what to do with his monkey.
He red-starred Wilmot to Len Hand. After
the initial shock, Len showered him with
affection. He made room for Wilmot on his
study desk at the University. But sadly,
when Len looked into Wilmot's eyes, he
could see that he carried a torch for
someone else. That someone was Amanda.*

Christine and I were out the bath and
just having brunch when Arthur dropped
by. He was in a terrible state.

"The Inland Revenue are after me."

His partner had been ripping him off for
years.

"Christ! We split up five years ago!
Simpleton! I hate the shit."

Simpleton and Arthur had had a cowboy
mending company, T.I.T. Services. Armed
with sticky tape and pocket screwdrivers,
Simpleton had roared their twenty-year-old
van into coughing life every morning.
They'd shoot off to work with Arthur
drooling over a cigarette and splashing
brown coffee down his stained trouser
fronts. Simpleton would drop Arthur at the
job in hand and tell him to start work while
he went back to the office to do some paper
work or make estimates for up and coming
jobs. Arthur did what he was told while
Simpleton went back to bed for a few

hours.

"I hate the shit!" Arthur said again.

"I hated the shit as well" Christine said. "He was a letch. I caught him looking up Shirley's skirt as she was climbing the stairs one day. He fancied her like a bee. Shirley used to be quite a honey."

"She'd have nothing to do with Simpleton. The bastard!" Arthur was quite upset.

"He spread rumours that wrecked Shirley's reputation for years. He played with her head something awful."

This Simpleton bloke sounded a right fiend.

"Head games were Simpleton's kink." Arthur muttered over a cup of tea.

"He screwed over you and Jean good," Christine informed me. "Jean loved him so much, she handed everything over to him. She worked as a schoolteacher. After three years with Simpleton, she hadn't a penny to show. Everything went into T.I.T. Enterprises."

Arthur was looking sick.

"Jean was the finance. Arthur was the labour. And Simpleton was a dead loss." Chris turned to Arthur. "Isn't that right."

"He kept the books, did the estimates, paid everybody except that he never did. No-one ever saw a penny."

They all parted on bad terms. Now the Inland Revenue were after them for tax evasion. Jean and Arthur thought that Simpleton had taken care of all that. The lying toad!

"All my friends are little froggies!" I said

to Christine.

"Twenty three thousand!" Arthur despaired.

"How much!" I asked aghast.

"Twenty three thousand quid!" Arthur put his head in his hands. "The bailiffs have just been around at my place with a summons. I've seven days to find twenty three thousand quid."

"What about Jean?" Christine asked.

"I've been to see her. She said that they're threatening to take away her house. I'll kill Simpleton!"

"I haven't seen him for five years" Christine said.

"I haven't seen him for three" said Arthur with a clench of his fists.

"I think I'd probably punch him in the face if I saw him." said Christine putting her hand on Arthur's shoulder.

"I'd kill him, Chris! He used me, the swine!"

I felt really sorry for Arthur. He's poorer than I am. He's got nothing of any value. He's on the dole like four million other people.

"I'll go to jail," he said.

"No you won't" Chris comforted him.

"I'm sick. I don't know what to do!"

I felt like giving Arthur a couple of quid, but it seemed ridiculous in the light of twenty three thousand. Christine gave him a hug instead.

"Get a solicitor, Arthur. It's do or die."

"I feel like dying," he said.

"You're only twenty eight. Death's for old people." Christine was really trying to get him ready for the fight.

"I've got grey hairs."

"Who hasn't, Arthur? At least you're not bald."

That sort of statement from Christine didn't seem to help at all. He left shortly after. Christine rushed off to her office saying, "I've just got to get this down." I carried on finishing my brunch.

AMANDA AND EDWARD

Amanda was a wonderful girl,
She could sing and dance.
She took when she could –
And had with her man
All the sex he advanced.

"I don't like it, Teddy."

"But, Mandy poohs" Edward teased, "We've done eve'ything else."

"I'll not have it in the kitchen."

"But we've known each othe' six yea's now." His grin made his moustache curl up his nostrils.

"I hate it when you're like this!"

"But Amanda, love of my life, desi'e of my hea't ... you'e such a sweet cunt."

"Screwing, balling, and fucking. What else do we ever do together?"

"It's these moments that keep us together. O big mama!" Admittedly, Amanda was a big girl. "Like the F'ench, it's the diffe'ences I like."

"You're drooling again" Amanda said curtly.

"Hi ho, Silve'!" shouted Teddy as he

attempted to mount Mandy.

"I can't handle you anymore" she screamed with a forelock that hooked Teddy to the floor. "I think it's time we split up."

"It's that damned monkey!" Edward grieved with a wail and a moan.

"You never found him for me, did you" Amanda, throwing open a cupboard in the kitchen, snarled, "Where's your suitcase?"

"What? What's happening?"

"You're leaving, Teddy. You're out on your lughole."

The lights around Brixton dimmed, and in the lee of the alleys, cats smoked ganja to escape their old ladies.

The one thing that annoyed me about Christine was that she was always writing. Her writing came before everything else. I mean, she said she loved me, but deep down I knew that her love for me was secondary to her love for her words. When she told me what her Mum had always wanted her to be, part of me wished that she had turned out like that. It was crushing to think that ball points and paper stood between Christine and me.

Well, that's how I saw it.

Christine didn't view it that way. It was her ambition, her drive and her way of making her mark on the world. At first I thought it was great ... living with the greatest undiscovered talent in the whole of England. I mean, I really wanted her to succeed, be great. But after awhile I realised that I mustn't also forget about myself. It was easy for me to revolve around Christine and her fantasy world, but underneath I resented that she didn't revolve around me. I wanted to be centre of the attraction, I wanted her affection, but all I got was words.

"My Mum always wanted me to be a dress maker," she told me after emerging from a three-hour exile in her office. I had been out getting the shopping, noticing the people rioting in the streets, and all that sort of real stuff. "She thought that with such a skill I could get a job in the costume department of a theatre and manage to meet famous people." I had just seen someone famous opening the new meat counter down at the supermarket. "It took me years to realise that meeting famous people was more important to Mum than being famous oneself." I reckoned that to be famous one had to be into one's self. "What chance did a girl have of being famous unless she was an actress, my Mum would say." I picked up the newspaper and read that the female Minster of Health had called the people in Newcastle 'ignorant'. "From an early age it was obvious that I would be no actress. I couldn't lie to save myself." The Iraqi's and Iranians were still bombing one another. "In Mum's eyes, dressmaking was the next best thing." The Israelis were still bombing the Palestinians. "If you haven't got the talent to be famous, then use your talent to make the famous need you."

Christine babbled on. Her Mum's logic seemed a bit vertical. Where were the hungry mouths of Bangladesh? I couldn't quite make out what famous had to do with happiness.

"Mum always told me that fame brings richness and respect. If you're rich, then you have everything you need." I hope she meant materially. "If you're respected, then you have everything you want from people" she meant emotionally " ... give or take a few broken hearts." Suddenly I had a flash of Soweto sear through my mind. "In a nutshell, you should be happy because you don't have to struggle. All you've got to do is keep working at being famous."

I felt a great wave of pity roll over me. Christine was indoctrinated. I suddenly felt that it was my task to re-educate her. Her Mum had got it almost right, but she had forgotten about the most important aspect of being an individual - being you. But then Christine surprised me by saying "I didn't want to be an actress or a dress maker. Mum could never see my side of it. I wanted to be a great poet."

Well, I couldn't help but admire Christine's fortitude. I mean, what had I done with my life. Bummed my way around the world for almost ten years with not a thing to show but thin blood and a tan all over. I had no great ambition to be somebody or something. Sure, I was important to myself but not to others. I was second best to them.

When I told Christine how I felt, she put her arms round me.

"I'm second best too," she said.

I asked her what she meant.

"I've settled for being a novelist," she said quite sadly.

"I love you for what you are." I said in reply.

I did love her for what she was. But it was hard for her to understand this because she wanted to be loved as a poet and novelist. My love of her was secondary to the worlds' love of her writing. Somehow I had to make her understand that I was more important to her than a whole universe of fame. Life was ticking on. She was thirty and nothing stopped time. I had to make her see that she couldn't spend all her life shut away in a tiny room writing for a public that did not exist.

"I still write poems" she said, "I think I've got six hundred in my tea-chest."

I thought about that for a moment and then said "Well, that's enough. Put down your pen, and let's go and make some love." The fame could wait but I couldn't.

JEANIE

Teddy Nobody of Brixton was actually a really nice bloke. In fact, he is living with Jeanie Redhead, a wild Scottish girl who met Teddy while he was looking for Wilmot.

Jeanie was one of those girls that hitch-hiked everywhere. Glasgow - M6 – London – M1 – Glasgow – M8 – Edinburgh – A1- London – M4 – Bristol – M5 – M6 – Glasgow - A74 - A69 – Newcastle – A1 – London – M1 – M6 - Glasgow ... Her lifestyle was routine, until she got a ride from a Truckee on the M6. He was driving across the water to Ireland.

For Jeanie, it was instant lust. For Francis O'Shea it was Christmas. They spent the night in a B+B in Holyhead and caught the afternoon sailing to Dun Laoghaire. That evening they got drunk in the Fleet Bar, Dublin.

But when Jeanie woke up the next morning in a grotty hotel near Mountjoy Prison, Frances O'Shea had opened his present and scampered. He had left her an Irish five-pund note, and a small boyish note in big scrawling letters CENSORED.

If it had not been for Sean O'Stage, an up and coming Kerry playwright who met Jeanie crying by the banks of the Liffey ... then heaven knows what might have become of the poor lass. The soft-hearted thespian writer took her trouble-free to Dun Laoghaire and bought her a ticket for Liverpool. He gave her twenty pounds for the onward journey which she spent M53 – M56 – M6 – M1 - London. She was so grateful she sent him a thank you letter, and in return, he made her the heroine of his next play.

In my own way, I was settling in at Christine's. I didn't have anywhere of my own that I could really call home. I had been on the road too long. I had never found that little piece of England that I could honestly say was mine. In some ways I envy those individuals who are brought into this world in the bedroom of a tiny cottage in the English countryside, and who, for one circumstance or another, never find reason to move away from their birthplace. They are the ones who truly inherit the earth. The rest of us are just wanderers who move from suburb to suburb, town to town and county to county. Yet, the individual who moves country to country suffers the worse and by far most painful dis-inheritance. This has been my fate.

Out of nostalgia, rather than from some great thirst, I bought some Darjeeling orange pekoe and took it home to Christine. In my heart I have the tender feelings for India. It is there, in that far distant giant that I came of age. In Delhi, in Darjeeling, in Madras, I spent the last days of my adolescence. If I am English, then, for many years I have felt an alien. Twenty-one in India. Twenty-three in Africa. Twenty-four in South America. Twenty-six and seven in the U.S.A. Twenty-eight in India again.

So, I had bought some orange pekoe in the indoor market. Somehow, I had to recapture a part of those years. I had decided that they were over. Something inside had died.

"O what a sweet boy!" Christine exclaimed when I gave her the tea. She kissed me and suddenly produced a package for me. "I've bought some black cherry from the same stall!" We boiled the kettle and had a pot of each. As usual, Chris was busy with her writing. I felt like talking about how I felt inside but it seemed the wrong time. She was in a really good mood and it didn't seem right to off-load my blues on her. She was wrapped up in the fantasy of her latest character, Sean O'Stage. I never knew if these people really existed or not. I mean, she was going on about some Irish playwright while I was sitting there getting flashes of the time I sold hot-dogs on Bourbon Street, New Orleans. She was comparing O'Stage to fellow Irishmen Sheridan, Shaw, Wilde, Beckett, O'Casey, and Arden ... while I was off floating with Tennessee Williams and William Faulkner.

SEAN AND URSULA

Sean O'Stage's play Jeanie took Dublin by storm. They played it at the Abbey for six months. It was the turning point of O'Stage's life. From dressing in jeans and an old pair of second-hand tennis shoes, he could now afford to run an old banger and eat at pizzerias. He began hobnobbing with Irish high society.

A certain young widow, who, it is reputed, had poisoned the wine of her late and senile peer of a husband for the estate and waning fortune, tried to lure O'Stage to her castle. She wanted him to write a play about her. O'Stage, a man of newly acquired experience, took up the challenge. Quitting his Glasnevin lodgings, he moved to the spacious comfort of Lady Usher-Forster's cat-guarded bed.

The view from the bedroom window was magnificent, overlooking as it did, some of the finest vistas in all Ireland. To awake every morning to such grandeur was *exulting. He did find the lions that stared down from the corners of the four-poster bed a trifle disconcerting. Lord Usher had been very keen on big game, and had bagged his fair share out in the colonies. Of course, Ireland had been an independent nation since 1922, but without compromise, the Usher-Forster's had been independent since George the Third. The death of Lord Usher, number sixteen, was entered in the family records as DIED OF INTOXICATION, reign of QUEEN ELIZABETH THE SECOND.*

Lady Usher-Forster was something else. She was always last to come to bed and first to rise. O'Stage woke every morning to breakfast being placed in his lap by the lady of the house. With a swish of the drapes, she would let the Irish dawn flood into the room. Throwing aside her night attire, she would ritually exercise and workout the excesses of the night. She would finish with twenty salutations to the sun, then quickly dress, and be off for her early morning ride. O'Stage, a man of slow urban lifestyle, would be barely out of bed before she returned to start on the paper work. The management of the estate occupied most of her working day, and O'Stage would see little of her until evening. By that time he was expected to have done his own work.

At dinner Lady Ursula would enquire how O'Stage's play was progressing. She had spared him no detail about her life and loves. Her talk was full of intimacies. She was a frank open woman, and O'Stage thought that she really was the most fascinating person he had ever met. Yet, despite the comfort of her hospitality, and the glorious divinity of her body, he was uninspired to write. The play remained unwritten.

"But Sean" she despaired when each night brought no further progress "if you can write about a whore, then surely you can write about a lady?"

O'Stage was full of excuses. At the back of his mind was the thought that she had murdered her husband. His talent had dried right up and he was frightened that she was going to do away with him. Yet somehow he couldn't believe that she had it in her to kill Lord Usher. Every time she spoke of him it was with kindness, but maybe that was because he had left her so much.

"I'm sorry, Ursula" he said "but sometimes it's not that easy to come up with a masterpiece just like that. You know I think you are absolutely wonderful in a thousand ways. I just can't find anything wrong with you that would be dramatically interesting."

On hearing this, Lady Ursula took him upstairs and fucked his legs off. "You know" she said "I've had my portrait painted, and that proved to be no problem for the artist."

The portrait hung above the fireplace in the drawing room. O'Stage had to admit that it was an exquisite masterpiece. He started to doubt his own talent. He had writer's block. For some reason he did not want to write about Ursula. He didn't want their relationship to end. At the root of his block, he was so utterly happy at Castle

Kildunny, he never wanted to leave the house of Lady Usher-Forster. She had enchanted him.

In sheer desperation, the young widow offered O'Stage so much money to write the play that his writer's block was overcome. Amid tears and shots of Gaelic coffee, he wrote the play in two days. Within a week it was being rehearsed at the Abbey, and before the month was out, it opened to a fanfare of expectation and speculation. Out of aristocratic integrity, Lady Usher-Forster refused O'Stage's plea to sit with him through the opening performance. In fact she wrote and told him that she could not come to the Abbey at all and that it would be impossible for them to meet again. She wished him well, and said that she was sorry that he had finally settled on a price for their love. Without the play they had been friends. Money or play, what had they mattered, she had loved him.

Now it was too late. THE LADY IN THE CASTLE flopped disastrously.

Sean O'Stage's reputation ruined, he left Ireland for America.

If only Christine and my love were so simple. I'm still working it out. But love affairs are always like that. How many have I had? Three real ones, five mediocre, twenty lukewarm, and two dozen one-night stands? I don't know. Time takes its toll. Christine?

"How many affairs have you had, Chrissy?"

"Mind your own business."

"It is my business, isn't it?" I mean to say, that was a dumb brush-off if I ever heard one. "Come on, Christine, be fair. I don't hold back anything from you."

Have you ever noticed that the deeper you get into an affair the less willing you become to tell the truth? I mean, it has to be forced out of the other person or you never get anywhere. Sometimes you don't have to pry; you have a relationship with someone who talks about his or herself non-stop. At first I thought Chrissy was like that, but as time went on, I realised that she was really quite a closed-off person. She put everything into her writing, but what came out wasn't the real Christine. It was a sort of fantasy. It was more how she would like to be, or at least, some of her stories reflected parts of her that never surfaced.

Underneath all her talk, Chrissy was really quite a romantic. Sure, deep down we all like to convince ourselves that we are the most romantic people in the world, but in truth, most of us are as conservative as shit. I'm not going to get down and grovel about my choice of words. Unlike Chrissy, I'm no poet. But I've been around long enough to know that romantic people are dreamers. We can forget about all the go-hard get-ahead types of folk who grab all the money and all the wealth.

None of those types of people are romantic.

The average Joe-shit spends all his time trying to be go-hard get-ahead to get a piece of the pie, but deep down, every single Joe is a dreamer.

They're romantics.

But when it comes to romance, Mr. Go-get Hard-Head and Mister Joe-shit Get-hard are just the same; they're as blue as bottle-flies on cow-turds. I mean, what is romance, but sweet smelling things and strange exotic notions that the wooed knows neither as real or imagined. Romance is airy and clouded in mystic, not hairy and covered in dog shit.

In her writing, Chrissy was a mixture of the airy and the hairy. As a person she was a mystery to me. That was the part I loved, the bit I knew nothing about. There was something in her conversation with me that she never talked about. It took months and months to work it out, but one day it hit me.

"You've been married. Haven't you?"

She looked at me with an expression of shock. She lay on the bed without saying a word, then burst into tears. At long last I'd pulled a nail right out of her sealed up past.

MORE ABOUT URSULA

Lady Usher-Forster with all the wealth she needed now had the notoriety of ruining Ireland's most promising playwright. The gossip columns were full of her imaginary conquests, and half the literary retainers of the Irish Arts Council courted her patronage.

She entertained none of them.

Instead of playing Diana to the crude

prying urbanite hacks and hangers-on of plebeian Dublin, Ursula took to the roads. She had re-discovered the thrill of fast cars. She sped about the environs of County Dublin like a joy rider. Because of her born-to-the-manor-do-as-she-pleased life-style, she had never bothered to take a driving test. Further, she had never concerned herself with the formalities of the commonest laws - driving license, insurance and road tax. These were in-roads on personal liberty that wealth circumvented.

When stopped at police roadblocks, the Guardia only had to take one look at Lady Usher-Forster to know that she was above their authority. Her very personality revealed that she knew the police commissioner, the mayor, and half the judges on the High Court bench. With a "Watch out for crazy joy riders, missus" they would always wave her on with a smile.

As a result, policemen like Copper McCafferty had to make his summons quota up in other ways. He had to lay twenty summonses a week on lawbreakers. On a good week he'd manage thirteen, fourteen ... He was always short.

McCaffery had to make them up.

Consequently, Barry McCann of the Ballymun Campsite became one of the most wanted men in Dublin. At the last count, Copper McCafferty had issued one hundred and twenty three summonses on Barry McCann. These, when added to the four thousand three hundred and sixty nine summonses issued on Barry McCann of

Ballymun Campsite by officers of the Dublin police force, made McCann a Will o'the Wisp. In the light of the seven hundred thousand summonses that had been issued throughout the Republic that year, it was a smart Dublin clerk who noted that there were only three and a half million people in all Ireland. There were either a legion of McCann's, a lot of lawbreakers, or it was a crime to sneeze. The imagination of the police was another one of those emerald isle facts.

Barry McCann had never stayed at the Ballymun Campsite in his life. Sure, everyone knew the travelling McCann's ... Willie, Tommy, Eamon, Joe, Eddie, Brian, Mickey, Pat, Colum, Fergus, Niall, Jimmy, Bart, Johnnie ... Aye, they'd all stayed at the Ballymun Campsite, except Barry.

"O Louis, I can't continue any more!"

Sheer and utter despair, that's the only way that I can describe it. Christine was cracking up. Well, sort of. She was clutching her head and staring at a letter.

"Another rejection."

I read the letter.

> Dear Miss Keemun,
>
> Thank you for letting me read your manuscript *The Cardboard Cowgirl*. I enjoyed it very much but feel that we cannot handle it. Unless you are American or have had your manuscript previously published in America, then I feel that no British publisher is likely to touch The Cardboard Cowgirl. We think your writing is against the present grain

of British publishing. While we do not doubt the sincerity of the writing, we do feel that it is not realistic. We might suggest that your talents could be better put to writing heavy romance like Catherine Cookson or Barbara Cartland.

Somehow I had to find words to bring Chrissy back into the world of the living. I mean, who were Catherine Cookson and Barbara Cartland?

"It's only a temporary set-back, pet," I said "These people haven't a clue what the public want."

Christine just sat there staring out the window at the redbrick walls of the terraced row of flats across the street. I could see her whole world deflating like a bald tyre.

"They can't go on ignoring you." I said.

"All she mumbled was "TThhh....."

"What was that?" I asked. I knew what she was going to say; I heard it every time a rejection arrived. It was her mantra back to sanity.

"Thirteen years!"

She was coming round.

"My god, Chris, if it takes another thirteen years you have got to stick with it. The more defeat, the sweeter the victory when it comes. Look what happened to King Alfred." I knew I had made the silliest of comparisons. Sometimes I'm not very bright.

It made her laugh though. "You see" I continued, "I always think about that Scottish king ... Robert the Bruce, you know, the one that watched the spider try and try again. Likewise, you've got to keep trying. You don't want to end up as just a wifely or something. Where's the fun in that?"

Of course I was thinking mainly of myself at that point. I didn't fancy Chrissy turning into a piece of household blubber. I mean, I quite liked the idea of her being a famous novelist, with me, the dark man in her life ... the sane driving force behind her ... fobbing off the hangers-on. It wouldn't exactly be the life of a Lady Usher-Forster, but anything had to be better than living in a run-down flat in a red-bricked terraced street in depressed northern England.

"And anyway" I continued, "*The Cardboard Cowgirl* is not one of your best, is it?"

Christine took in a deep breath and said "No." Then she changed her mind. "O I don't know." I thought she was going to cry. "They don't want American epics written by non-Americans. I've got two!"

It was all too much. The emotion was filling up the room and gushing down the stairs. I had to open the window, but the smell from the brewery down the street made me close it doubly quick. Christine was lying face down on her desk in a coma. I had to get some air into her somehow.

"My agent says my writing is against the present grain of British publishing," she sobbed. I had to pump her with hope fast.

"No wonder I don't buy novels in this country!" I declared.

In truth, I couldn't remember the last novel I'd bought?

I had to put a word in for the lefties to qualify my statement.

"Novels in this country are all about people just down from Oxbridge." Saying that made me feel really good. At long last I thought I'd hit the right note to revive Chrissy.

"They're right, Louis. I'm against the grain."

But it was too late. I wasn't listening to Chrissy anymore. I was on my high horse trampling down British writers and publishers.

"The British novel died with Jane Austen! They've been telling the same story for a hundred years. Novel, I ask you!" I said in disgust. "They're as old as gas lighting."

When I turned round to face Chrissy, she was still lying with her head on her desk. There was nothing I could do. There lay thirteen years that I knew nothing about. Then all of a sudden, she sat bold upright. It was really peculiar. One second she was lying like a rag doll, and the next, she was the Chrissy I loved and cherished.

"Make us a cup of tea, luv" she said.

It was quite astonishing. I was so relieved; I did what I was told. I knew that by the time I came back from the kitchen, she'd be well into part seventeen of her latest novel.

BARRY THE TINKER

Barry McCann, the terror of Dublin, lived like Don Quixote. As big-hearted as a windmill, he took things on a whim. He loved to sing.

> Tinker, tailor, soldier, sailor,
> I wander the wide green world.
> I take what I can with a sleight o' hand.
> I spirit away silver and gold.
> I sleep in the hay from June to May.
> I dance along the Emerald Isle roads.
> Since I was a lad, I've always had
> Stars in my eyes, rings in my ears.
> I never worry about where I'm going.
> I laugh when its sunny, sing when its
> snowing.
> I'm Barry McCann ... born to die roving.

Barry's favourite town was Derry. It was a fine old place. Yet sometimes he thought that the people there were the unhappiest folk. To be sure, there was always some trouble. Then again, the trouble was the Troubles.

Whenever Barry's light-finger-ness got him into trouble on one side of the town, he'd cross the River Foyle to the sanctuary of the other. No one ever followed him. You see, the Protestants never went to the Catholic east side. Similarly, the Catholics never crossed to the Protestant west bank.

Barry was an atheist. As a pagan he was unwanted by either side.

Derry was the only town Barry knew where the people couldn't make up their mind what the town was called. There was such bitterness over the name Londonderry ... the Catholics hated it because of the Brits, the Protestants branded it because they were British ... that the townspeople *to smooth over the Troubles called their urbs hibernia 'City by the Foyle'.*

Barry had been born in the Bogside in a caravan, but he was neither Unionist nor Republican. He was a tinker. His mother and father had been travellers, and as a result, Barry had never gone to school. The 3R's were no good to travellers, especially the first R. His inability to read meant that he had a plausible excuse to ignore KEEP OUT signs and NO TRESSPASSING notices. The only relative of Barry's who had learnt even the first 2R's had gone to America.

Life at Chrissy's flat was getting boring. I lay in bed a lot trying to decide what to do next. I mean, I'd been to all these countries around the world and nothing had really happened. Well, things had happened, but nothing that drastically changed my life. Anyway, nothing drastic I could remember at the time.

I was becoming a vegetable. Christine had her writing to keep her from going nuts. Sure, she cracked up every now and again when she got a rejection or something, but I mean, that all came to the surface. Funnily enough, contrary to what I had thought about Chrissy before I really got know her, she was really quite normal. I was the weird one. One day this idea just came into my head and it wouldn't go away.

"Chris! I've decided," I said.

"Decided what, Louis?"

"We're going around the world."

"Are we?"

"I've made up my mind. Are you coming?"

"When? How?"

"We'll go next month!"

"But, Louis?"

"It's now or never, Chris. This time I want to go East to West. There's nothing here for us in this place. It's emptier than Eliot's wasteland. It's all thistles and rosebay willow herb. Stuff the idle English. Are you coming or not?"

"Well, I don't know, Louis. It's all rather quick."

"Better a quick end than a slow death." I often defended myself with totally irrelevant phrases. "Well?"

"It's so..."

"It's settled then!"

"But what about my novel? So far it is set in Britain and Ireland. It'll change dramatically if we start travelling."

She had a point, but who cares about reading about boring old Britain when there is a whole sphere of wonder out there.

"You've been to America," I said.

"You've been to Morocco," I continued.

"So what" I stated emphatically "It won't make you the greatest writer in the world.

I paused.

"You've got to experience things, Chrissy. This staying in your office seven days a week is a waste of time. You've got to go out and find out what the rest of the world is doing before you can really understand what is going on in your own world. I mean, it is all very well writing about the Barry McCann's of this world, but that is really the extent of your knowledge. The only way you found out about Barry McCann was because of that writers' tour of Ireland you went on with that feminist group you got involved with."

"I've been to India" she said.

"You went to India for three weeks when you graduated from college and you got the Old Toda story. But apart from that, you don't really know much else."

I thought she was going to hit me at this point. I changed course.

" Well, maybe you know a little bit about people, but how much can you write without the same characteristics surfacing in each of your stock characters. I mean, I like Len Hand, the Perverted Monkey Lover, but how many more weirdoes like that can you dig up. You seem to have a problem writing basic down-to-earth stuff about the Smiths and Jones and the neighbours next door. Everything you scribble down seems to be a sort of fantasy."

This brought me back to Chrissy living out her world on paper.

"You've got to get out of this bloody office and go and lose yourself in a jungle or something. I've done it and it hasn't done me any harm."

As soon as I had made that last statement I knew I'd left myself wide open. I thought I was about to be ripped to pieces. But the love of my life looked at me in a quiet sort of way, took my hand, and led me to the bedroom. Taking off all my clothes and kissing me all over, she whispered softly

"What will I do with my tea-chest?"
I turned over on to my stomach and said
"Stick it up my arse."

PATRICK

*Patrick McCann owned a bar in New
York. He called it 'The Enniskillen Turncoat',
but everyone else called it Paddy's. Unlike
other Irish-Americans, Paddy did not serve
green beer on St Patrick's Day. He thought
it was a disgusting habit.*

*"'Mericans tar heat'ens" he said. "I tink
all beer shoud b' black."*

*Paddy was one of the few publicans in
America.*

*"'Mericans ar all beer swillerz" he said.
"Ow many barmun in dis country kno tat
serving beer iz a ritual, not an art."*

*His accent was shot to hell, but there
was poetry in Patrick's speech. The McCann
blood ran deep.*

*"Me ehol famly wer gypsies. I wiz
brought up wi' the leprechauns and politics.
We had a start on 'em all, the fairies wer on
owr side!"*

*Paddy's bar was always full. He sold
beer on tick and cashed welfare checks. He
was honest, though.*

*"A nevr took a penny frum a mun hu
couldn't afford tit."*

*He sometimes lied through his teeth.
Not regularly, but often enough.*

*"Ecxaggerashun. Tis in me blood to go
over the top fur a bit of crack. Grand
license. Hurms no-one."*

Then, as if completely off the top of his

head, he said
"Peepul lik Bugs Bunny ar a screem."
Paddy got to meet Bugs Bunny when he went to Anaheim on a brewery conference. In reality, behind the costume, Bugs was Jose Hernandez, an illegal alien from Tabasco.

And so we began travelling. Chrissy could no longer constrain her novel; she was mentally flying off to Mexico and the likes. Admittedly, on a human day-to-day level, it took us a while to get things together. God knows where the money came from. To tell the truth I did a little bit of hocus-pocus here and there. Christine didn't have a penny. But because this whole story is pocket-book fiction anyway, the practical realities of money can be dispensed with. Besides, money is boring. We wanted to escape all that and float away on a cloud.

"I want to float away on a cloud" said Christine.

"I'd rather go Lufthansa" I replied.

Instead of flying, we started out overland. We did a dummy run and spent a weekend in Blackpool. It coincided with the Labour Party Conference. The result of such bad planning was that we couldn't get on the big wheel at the fun fair because it was permanently occupied by delegations of socialists. It was all "By gum, mate!" "Bye heck, lad!" and "Och aye, man!" In its own way it was quite charming, but all you could get to eat on the front was hot-dog and chips.

The landlady at the boarding house was a sweet old soul. Her dinners of mince, chips, two veg, followed by apple pie or sponge pudding and custard were lapped up by the delegates' hungry from backslapping and boozing. Chrissy and I, your trendy veggies, were treated to mountains of steamed carrots and cabbage. As usual we alternated between egg rolls and cheese pasties. I looked forward to going back to Shree Krishna's Lunch Home for dossa and oothappam. Chrissy wanted to know what I was talking about, so I told her about this place in Madras. As I extolled the wonders of Shree Krishna's, she made a few notes, then wrote a poem

MADRAS

In a city famed for its cuisine,
And noted for dossa and bakala:
Between the savories and sweet things -
The bajis and gulabjamons ...
There is pongle, poori, and semia,
Noddles in a variety of sauce;
And the famous masala dossa,
Food for Koolie or God.

I had to admire Chrissy's ability to write at will. When we got back from Blackpool, the poem went into the tea chest. We had arranged for Alice to look after the tea chest while we went around the world. She thought we were crazy, but once she had mellowed out, she insisted that Chris had to write to her every day.

"Alice ... " Chrissy said with her arm around her friend "I am going to write everyday, and you are going to type out everything that I send back to you."

"What are you and Louis going to do for money?" she asked.

Back to that again. I've already explained to you that in fiction - money is something you just don't have to worry about. In reality, money is the one thing that stops people from travelling. I actually think that it is not that important. Trying to explain that to someone who counts his or her pennies every morning is impossible.

"I'll not trouble you with finances" Christine told Alice.

And I'll not trouble you with the labours of packing and saying goodbye to everyone. I mean, we just got on with it. Sure, we had our long goodbyes and all that bubbly nonsense, but I mean, we were only going around the world. I was certainly intent on coming back. After all, there were worse places than boring fascist capitalistic arse-licking forelock touching England. But I'll get to that.

Eventually, after more delays, and still more, we took off.

We were on our way ... we were as free as imagination allowed. Guess where we went first?

BUGSY JOE

Joe was really from Mazatlan.

"Soy un hombre a la cuidad" Joe told the world. *"Me gusto mucho a trabahar en Disneyland. Todas dia quando tengo hambre. Prendo a comer hamburgers,*

*french fries, milkshakes. Pero, me corazon
es in Mexico donde mi esposa vive. Bebo
mucho dinero et las muchachas son mi
major amigos. Pero, soy felix.*

Joe was hard to understand unless you
spoke Spanish, or unless you got so
completely drunk that everything he said
made sense. He owned a '68 Catalina which
had been rear-ended, but that didn't bother
Joe. The Pontiac got him from Buena Park
to Anaheim and back every day. He shared
the gas and an apartment with Donald
Duck. Sometimes Joe and the Duck would
cruise up and down Hollywood Boulevard in
their costumes in the hope of attracting
some attention.

But it was the girls in leotards on roller
skates, and fat old cats in Mercs and
Rollers, who turned the heads and got the
come ons.

"Them guys should stick to the Strip
bunny clubs" moaned the Duck.

"Yo no comprendo Norte Americanos"
Joe would say. Despite all the drawbacks of
being a second-class citizen in California, he
liked the U.S. It was part of his job as Bugs
to do commercials. One time he'd been sent
out to Imperial Valley to promote vegetable
produce. He was photographed sitting on
top of a mountain of carrots. The next he
knew, he had been blown-up and pasted on
boards right across the States. The
photographer gave Joe a print of the
negative and he sent it to his wife in
Mazatlan.

I mean, Mexico, I ask you. It's one of

those places everybody's got to see. First impressions ... and all that. Chrissy was in her element. I hardly saw her. Well, I saw her, but we weren't communicating. She always seemed to have a pen in her hand and her nose in a notebook.

"Heh, Chris" I said "Instead of writing all this fictional crap, how about giving us a reading. Yes?"

"Why not" she said looking up for the moment. She looked radiant in the sub-tropical shade. We were in a little town called San Felipe at the northern end of the Gulf of California. "Yes, why not" she said again "Now's as good a time as any."

"What are you going to tell them, then?" I asked. Them, of course, are you's, the ordinary Joe's and Johanna's, the common John's and Jane's. You see, I was setting it up, trying to get Chrissy to come out of herself. I wanted her to throw her rotten oozing pen away. I had developed this little game with her. I would pretend that I was her audience at one of those writing circle readings, you know, those yawn provoking affairs where famous, and not so good, writers go along and read out aloud their latest piece of crap to a bunch of smiling back-stabbers.

"Naturally enough" Chrissy replied "I'll tell them about the beauty of Mexico. No, wait a minute; I've had a creative flash. I'll tell them the story of the One Minute Traveller in Mexico.

"What?" I asked. Once again having started Chrissy talking, I began to think that it wasn't such a good idea. I mean, we were in this little place called the Hotel Iris. San Felipe was a dusty little costal town wedged between the sierras, the desert, and the Gulf. A colony of pelicans were blackening the sky just beyond the cliffs out of town. It was quite a sight. I had been used to seeing pelicans awkwardly paired or alone. The vision of thousands, and I mean thousands of pelicans, falling out of the sky and plunging recklessly upon waters silver with fish, is one of these wonders of nature you see three times a day on television but never in real life. I thought, maybe Chris would write about such imagery, but no, that would have been too easy.

"I don't think they'd believe you" I said "No-one goes to Mexico for one minute. One minute travellers to Mexico are a myth."

"Do you want to hear it or not." It was like an ultimatum.

"Okay, but I don't think you'd get away with it." A story about a one-minute traveller to Mexico sounded like a cheap joke.

THE ONE-MINUTE TRAVELLER IN MEXICO

Bob and Phil had been at a loose end all day. It was Sunday, and it was hot, the hottest Veterans Weekend they'd both ever known. For November, it was eighty degrees on the edge of the Southern Californian desert. The lush Imperial Valley was waiting for the winter rains. It was lettuce-planting season, and there would be no more work unless the rains came.

The boys, thirsty from smoking marijuana, quenched the dry of their raw throats with cokes from a vender. They gazed across the arid landscape to the mirage horizon. The town was quiet. The streets were always ghostly on the Sabbath. Yet, no bells tolled to remind the citizens of El Centro of their responsibility to God. In a way it was eerie.

The kindly minded boys thought the day no different from any other. El Centro had always been dead. The lady in the candy store had died years ago. Even the town undertaker had died years back.

Chrissy suddenly stopped.

"Eh, this bit about the undertaker side-tracks the story too much. I'll jump a section and continue."

ONE MINUTE TRAVELLER IN MEXICO
PART TWO

Picking lettuce was big money in the Imperial Valley. Having to wait around for the rains was costing Bob and Phil eighty bucks apiece every day. They spent the time drinking in the bars and playing pool. Phil, by Californian law, was to young to drink, but there was nothing else to do. He walked around without I.D. so he could drink. Bob was always reminding him that it was also against the law to be on the streets without any I.D. But it was no big deal. There were so many illegal Mexicans in El Centro, the cops never hassled the Caucasian boys.

El Centro was only ten miles from the Mexican border. Bob was bored out of his head. After a few more joints, the thought of going down to the chicken wire to have a look at Mexico seemed better than spending the rest of the day in fried El Centro. They strolled down to the bus station and asked the clerk how they'd go about going down to the border town of Calexico.

The clerk was also the bus driver. He let them ride free to Calexico in the smoking section. When they arrived in Calexico they thought they were already in Mexico. They might as well as been, everyone in Calexico was Mexican. The driver put them down in the bus station opposite the border crossing. He gave them some free returns and reminded them that they needed I.D. if they wanted to cross into Mexico."

That left Phil out.

Bob, with a grin like a tortilla chip, showed his driving license, and passed through the turnstile in the chicken wire. No soon was he in Mexico than he turned round and came back to tell Phil what it was like.

"Man" Bob said, "You wouldn't believe it, Phil boy." He laid it on like peanut butter and jelly.

"You were only in Mexico a minute, you bull shitter" Phil said irately.

"As a One Minute Traveller to Mexico, I saw a whole universe of things I can tell you about on the bus back to El Centro. You'll never guess what happened to me in that one minute."

"Don't bullshit me, man," Phil answered.
"But it's true, Phil" Bob potato chipped
"I saw a whole universe."

"Is that it?" I asked.
"Guess so," she said, "It's my One Minute Traveller in Mexico story."
"It's off the top of your head," I said.
"No, I've written it down."
"Well" I said, "That's bloody pathetic. Why can't you write about the pelicans or something?"
"What pelicans?" she said.
"Those bloody things over there!" I pointed.
"You know" she said, "I thought they were seagulls."
I gave up for the day. I mean, what was the point. There we were in Baja, a place where saguaro cactus dominated the skyline. There was little else to do but watch the pelicans and frigate birds, and listen to sallow Mexican music. I looked back at Chrissy, and of course, she had her head back in her notebook. Then suddenly she caught my eye and burst out laughing. I went completely crimson. I felt like an innocent little boy when I suddenly realised that she had made up the story out of her head after all. It was such a wonderful feeling. There was now no one else in the whole world I would rather have been in Mexico with than Christine Keemun.

AFTER THE CARROT JOB

Photographer Jeremy Slimey took a long

vacation in Hawaii after the Carrot job. He couldn't find any solitude on Waikiki, so he flipped twenty dollars and flew over to Kauai. He hung around Lihue for a few days, but he soon got bored. He hired a car, and on the way to the north of the island he picked up a girl hitchhiker.

"I'm on my way to Paradise," she said.

"Gee, that's nice" Slimey said with a sickly smile.

"Everything's free in Paradise," the girl said warmly.

Slimey looked at the girl with a sly grin. He was just about to ask her if she'd fuck him when she said

"You have to take all your clothes off."

Completely thrown by the girl's statement, he didn't know what to say.

"Um ... can I come?"

The girl looked at him. To Slimey it seemed half an hour before she said anything. She sat there staring at him with the sort of blank look that all the young kids had when they were sizing him up. Slimey counted the white lines on the road.

"What you do for a living?" she asked.

"I'm a photographer," he said sheepishly. He pointed to his camera in the back.

"What do you photograph?" she asked.

"Flowers and things, you know," he said. The words whistled through his teeth and his nose grew longer than Pinocchio's.

The girl didn't notice. "Aw, that's all right. There's bunches of flowers and things in Paradise. The Group won't mind if you take your camera.

The Group. Slimey began to wonder what he'd have to go through to get laid. All he wanted to do was to get the girl on the beach and get his rocks off. She was no plum, but he was hardly a peach himself.

"My favourite is the Venus Flytrap," she said.

Slimey just grinned.

With his eyes on the road and the cliffs that dropped away on the right, the road wound past Hanalei beach.

"South Pacific was made here," she said. Slimey vaguely remembered a movie where happy hands did all the talking.

A few miles later the road ended at Haena.

"We get out here," she said.

She led him across the baking Haena beach littered with one-day tourists and started to scramble up the cliff face. Slimey, in thongs, boxer shorts, and tee shirt, held on to his beer gut as he wobbled up after her. After two miles of huff and sweat along an overgrown path, they descended into Paradise.

Paradise was a small cove with a white sandy beach hemmed in by towering volcanic cliffs that rose to four thousand feet. A waterfall tumbled out of the cliffs to create a stream that emerged at the bay to form a small fresh water lagoon kept apart from the sea by a narrow sandbar. Everywhere pink guavas dropped from the trees; isolated banana plants nestled in against the cliffs; prawns and fry darted in the fresh water. Pandana trees gave shade over smooth basalt rocks where freaks and

doo-la wasters had made homely shelters.
"This is Hanakapiai," the girl said.
Big signs hung from the guava trees.

NO NUDITY! NO CAMPING! NO MARIJUANA
SMOKING! NO LITTERING! NO SHITING! NO
NOTHING!

"Aw ... just ignore them" she said, "This
is Paradise."
Evening was coming on, and the sun
was finally dropping behind a low horizon of
cloud. Slimey and the girl sat naked by the
water's edge and talked about the clouds,
the sea, the emerging stars. They were
drawing closer to one another, and Slimey
was about to pop the question about
fucking, when suddenly he saw a group of
Park Rangers scrambling down the cliffs
towards the beach.
A cry went up like some exotic bird call
"Pee-arrs! Pee-arrs! Pee-arrs!" The girl
turned around and gasped.
"Git yer clothes, Gerry, and run!" she
shouted. It was all part of the fun of being
in Paradise.

Hawaii was okay. Well, it was a sort of
paradise. Chris's view of Hawaii was only
one side of the dime. There was five cents
not worth talking about. I mean, there were
some really weird people out there. For
example, take Sunflower. There we were,
Chrissy and me, in this tent in Kokee Park,
Waialeale, the wettest place in world. All
around us was tropical rain forest. We
weren't exactly in the wettest place in the

world ... that was five miles away. But naturally enough, it rained a lot. Chrissy was happy it rained, it reminded her of England. I mean, that was okay, but the rain endlessly came and went. Sure, when the sun came out after a downpour, the forest came to life - mynahs, mockers, cardinals, finches, and of course, the jungle fowl. These wild chickens would crow and sing like one big family choir. I mean, when the sun shone it was great, but when it rained ... which it did all the time, it wasn't so good. After about five days in the jungle of Kokee, the blues started to settle in.

Then Sunflower showed up with his flute. He looked just like Krishna, and my heavy attitude evaporated.

"I came to make my home in Kokee". It was almost as if he sang his words. "I came here to love the birds and the holy silence." As I said, Sunflower was a little strange. "I came to find my heart in Kokee."

I was sitting there wondering why he'd left San Francisco. Yet, there was something about the guy that was soothing. His mellow voice floated over the valley and filled the trees with joy so that all the birds stopped mid-song to listen to his flute.

"I see the morning, and I see the beauty in my home. I came to hear you, Wind. I came to feel you, Rain. I came to smell you, Flowers. I came to taste you, Fruit. I came to touch your hearts. I came to share your joy."

Chrissy, busy writing about Jerry Slimey suddenly stopped on the word 'Paradise'. She listened intently as Sunflower's flute

made more in-roads into the jungle than
the curling fire-smoke from our little camp.
All life fell still as Sunflower's music of love
brightened up the wettest place on Earth.

"God made you all; you tallest tree …
you little flower. We live in the valley of
love and peace. We all live as one."

Sunflower incanted into the afternoon,
and not once did it rain. It was a miracle.
He laid aside his flute, and took up his
violin.

It was bloody awful. Two inches of rain
fell in two hours.

It was back to normal. The clouds rose
up and over the Kokee jungle on the slopes
of volcanic Wai-al-e-al-e in the heart of
Kauai.

UNWELCOME

Chief Ranger, Captain Unwelcome,
hated welfare freeloaders. 'Eighty-eight-
dollars-a-month-bums' is what he called
them.

You see, Nat Unwelcome knew nothing
about nobody, and nothing about himself.
When he had been stationed in Belem
during the Second goddam War, he'd seen
the natives lolling about taking life easy
while he had slaved to help America win the
war.

"If it warn't fur uz buoys from the
States, thir'd be no goddam world fit fur
heroes and free men."

As you might have guessed, Nat hated
women … except his wife. He only loathed
her. When he had first met her in Rio whilst

on furlough, he thought that he had loved her.

"Brazilian tart! Good luker though befur she got hog-fat on junk food."

But he knew he was only fooling himself, or least, he might have reckoned she was a worse old lady than she had got for a husband.

"No good degos ... the goddam whoile continent. She brought all her no-good brothers owver to our beautiful white country ... had them livin' evurwhere ... An I mean evurwhere ... kitchen ... bathroom.

Nat exaggerated a lot.

"E's a non-good bullshitter!" Maria kept telling her eight sons when they had a good word for their Pop. "Y blame his modder, his Polish modder."

All the sons had long since grown up. They'd gone their own ways. Six of them lived on welfare, the eldest was in jail, and the youngest Joachim had gone to Brazil to escape the fate of his elder brothers. He had lived with his Mom's ancient parents in Belem for a while before drifting south to the bright lights of Sao Paulo and Rio.

Okay. At this point you might wonder how Chrissy and I got from Hawaii to Brazil after being in Mexico.

I still wonder too. I thought we were going east to west around the world, then West to East, but now we were just going anywhere. After that Sunflower bloke had tried to run off with her in Kauai while I was out for a walk in the Kokee jungle, I wasn't inclined to trust Chris as much as I did before. I mean, when the guy jumped on her and tried to do the dirty on her, she let him.

I know that sex is only sex, but it did kind of hurt. She was honest enough to tell me it had happened, but it was that weird Sunflower bloke who told me that they were heading out together and leaving me behind. I mean, if I hadn't treated the whole thing as a joke and laughed, and if Sunflower hadn't just at that moment fallen apart with guilt, I'm sure she would have gone with him.

So there we have it. Sure, you're only hearing my side of the story. You probably won't hear Chrissy's side for another five or ten years. Writers are like that ... they'll remember and record every detail of someone-else's life and put it down verbatim. But their own live? Not Chrissy. She's still a dark secret if you only read her writings. I suppose I know her better because I went around the world with her, I mean, people fall apart every-now-and-then, and Chrissy is no exception. I sometimes fall apart, but I'm likely to tell someone about it. Chrissy doesn't.

Somehow, we managed to stick it out. I kept expecting that any moment I'd get a glimpse of Chrissy's deeper emotions. But nothing ever surfaced. It was like looking for a reflection in the pitch dark. She never unlocked her heart long enough to let her imprisoned emotions out for a walk in the exercise yard. There were no visitor's days. She remained behind a solid stonewall. She was a Dartmoor, a Barlinnie, and an

Alcatraz, all rolled into one.

After the two-timing at Kokee, I was all for a parting of the ways. But Chrissy pleaded with me to forget all about it. It was just one of those wild spontaneous fucks she said. It was part of life. People came and went. You had to go with the flow and all that kind of crap. She was anything but remorseful.

Hell, I was in such a shit-hole fever I didn't know what I was doing in a piss-down Hawaiian jungle. I just broke down and cried. It was all so unfair. I mean, Chrissy was the one who should have been crying with guilt. She should have been begging me to forgive her. And did she? No, fricking way! She told me to grow up and face reality. She'd only screwed the guy. It was over.

It was so embarrassing. I mean, there were other people around. One guy felt so sorry for me, he came and stuck a big fat joint in my mouth. Looking back on it, I think that joint did more to bring together the shattered parts of my broken ego than any of Chrissy's peace making. But it mellowed me out so fast that, before I knew it, I had Chrissy back in my arms. God knows how she got there. She probably squirmed. She could be a right worm at times.

"Let's forget all this and go to Brazil," she said.

JOACHIM

In Rio, Joachim Unwelcome, made

welcome, worked the nightlife.

His command of English delighted the tourists. During the day he put his father's tongue to good use on the beaches of Copacabana and Leblon.

"Hi, Babe! Want a massage?"

"G'day. No way!" the girl replied. She was from ...

"Oz" Joachim guessed.

"Yeah, that's right, sport. How'd yu'know."

"Hay, I'm from Honolulu. I watch the T.V ... Shit, you've sure got some bad cop programs over there."

"You mean good?" she asked

"Hey, I ain't no Negro. When I say 'bad', I mean 'bad'."

"I think you need to sit in the shade, Bruce."

"Hay, missy Oz, don't tell me my business. Look, I like you, so I want to tell you a few things. Okay?"

"Shooo" Miss Oz said.

Joachim was getting the message that he wouldn't be massaging. He got up and began walking away along the beach towards Ipanema.

"Heh, Honolulu, where you going" Miss Oz shouted "I thought you were going to tell me a few things?"

"You told me to shoo!" Joachim shouted back.

"I said Sure. You know ... Fire away! I think you better come back, sport."

And that was that. Joachim and Miss Miranda Oz balled their way through the rest of the day and night.

Those long hot Rio days. Drinking tea in Maxims. Walking bare-footed up Corcovado. Those long hot Rio nights. Swimming naked in the waters of Guanabara Bay. Romancing to sweet samba song into the long twilight of the southern world in search of bliss.

Ecstasy.

Don't believe a word of it. Christine's a pure sham. The truth is something else. The days were rolling by. We'd pulled into a garage about KM380 on the Brasilia road with a flat. Chrissy had gone off in a huff because I'd told her off about telling lies. She'd told some guy that she was a famous novelist. I told Chrissy that she couldn't go around saying things like that. She wanted to know why. I told her the reason why though I shouldn't have needed to.

When Christine starts bragging I can't stand the sight of her. It's bad enough when she bullshits her way through the truth, but being a famous novelist ... she had gone too far. I reminded her that she'd never had one word of her prose published by anyone. I hit her softest spot. She didn't write another word until we got to Australia.

MIRANDA

Miranda Oz, the 'down-under' girl, went back to Hobart, Tasmania, with tales of South American life that no one believed. Frustrated at the incredulity of her 'been nowhere' compatriots, she began writing poetry that slammed the complacent billabong mentality that had fix-pegged her as "a rather strange Sheila".

You're all wallies and dingbats,
Marinos and dingoes ...

Powerful satire flowed off her cascading anger. She ripped at the fabric of Aussie society to reveal the innards.

Melbourne and Sydney,
the liver and kidney ...

Yet no one took her seriously. A Sheila writing verse? Yet ... there was one. Her parakeet Sparky. Sparky just loved his mistress's poetry. He'd come a long way from his days in the wild.

Chris and I were friends again. We had a barb and tinny time in Australia. I had an old friend who lived out in Cairns, Queensland. We made the long drive up from Sydney, and arrived just half-an-hour after my friend Jack had got back from China with his Hangchow wife. I polished up my Mandarin.
"Wo-laiguo-Zhongguo-jici dou-mei-quguo-Hangzhou" I said. "Xiwang-jianglai qu-yici."
"Yinwei-wo-xihuan-Hangzhou," said Jack's wife Lu "souyi-congqian-jiu-xiang, jianglai-wo-'yiding-zhao-yige-difang xiang-Hangzhou-yiyang-hao wo-cai-zhu-ne."
Poor Christine. She didn't understand a word. You see ... Hangchow is a very nice

place. Any Englishmen who travel to China feel that they must go there. When they all come back they rave on about how beautiful it is. Hangchow has a lake called West Lake. In the old days, people compared West Lake to Xi Shi, one of the greatest beauties in Chinese history. I mean, I'd been to China several times but I'd never been to Hangchow. However, when I got talking to Lu, I found out she was from Soochow. While Hangchow is famous for its scenery, Soochow is famous for its women. It's a bit like the thrifty Scotsman and the hard-bargaining New Englander. In China, the natives of Shansi are known to be penny-pinching, the Cantonese cunning, and the Soochow women beautiful.

"Is that so?" asked Chrissy jealously searching for that beauty in the face and movements of Lu. She couldn't see the same beauty Jack and I saw in Lu. But Lu was very tactful.

"Bu-yiding" she said. "Youde-piao-liang, youde-ye-hen-nan-kan."

"That's not true, Lu" said Jack. "Suzhou-nu-ren shi-piaoliang."

Later Jack told me that he had gone to Soochow because he'd heard the women were beautiful. He had always wanted a beautiful wife and he found Lu.

Jack was obviously deeply in love with her.

"There's an old saying in China about Soochow and Hangchow" Jack added.

Shang-you-tiantang (Above is Heaven)

Xia-you-Su-Hang   (Below are Soochow and Hangchow)

Lu and Chrissy just didn't get on. There was something in both their nature's that made them meet head on. Lu knew that Chrissy was a vegetarian, but she insisted on throwing bits of chicken into the vegetable chow mein. Chrissy, aware of Lu's poor English, talked at a rabbit's pace with Jack to exclude Lu from the conversation. Eventually Lu found out that Chrissy was writing a book.

"Ta-xiede-neiben-shu-yijing-'xiedao-nar-le?" she asked me.

"O, her novel? About a third."

"Ni-ba-neiden-shu   'dou-kan-wan-le-ma?" she inquired.

"I try and keep up with what she's writing. I think it's in Australia now. But I'm losing interest. I'm thinking of writing my own book."

And that was true. If Chrissy could make and mix up the truth in her book, why couldn't I? I mean, I was getting tired of reading about these fictional characters of hers. I ask you, who in their right mind could ever believe that Sparky the Budgie was for real.

It was utter nonsense.

SPARKY

Sparky was no ordinary budgie ... his ancestors had seen boomerangs fly the skies as black as vultures.

Somehow, Sparky's ancestors had

survived to pass on their fanciful tales to their progeny. Ayers Rock had been their homeland, his father's roost. Sparky didn't know much about his mother because budgie folklore was all about the males of the species.

Despite being a town bird, Sparky retained his pride. He never coyly pleased his tormentors with "Pretty boy!" and all that sort of human crap. He spoke his own language fluently and conversed well with other birds pitching-in in dialect from the other side of the double-glazing. He was no squawk, squeak, or squitter.

Sparky had a squint, but the way he looked at humans you could tell he thought that most humans were dumb. As a result, *his favourite trick was to bite them on the nose. It always put some life into them.*

"That's my boy!" his mistress Miranda would squeal when Sparky flew down from his cage to sit on visitors' heads. He would then hop onto a shoulder.

"Isn't it cheeky" the visitors would say with a turn of their heads to look at Sparky shitting on their shoulders.

"Watch out for ... " Miranda would start to say, but the warning always came too late. Sparky, going for the noses, always succeeded in drawing blood.

Frequently, in retaliation, the visitors would try to strike back, but Sparky was up-up-and-away. He was always too fast.

"Isn't he a wily wee thing" Miranda would grin in admiration. Her visitors were never amused. They all hated Sparky.

The greatest shock in Sparky's life came

when it was discovered that he was a she.

"He's got an orange bit on his nose, not blue" some Smart Snot said one day. "He's a girl!"

Being a girl budgie, there is no point telling you anymore about Sparky as budgie folklore is all about the males of the species.

The Smart Snot was a right Australian spoilsport.

We were in Aus quite awhile. Anyone who's been there can probably tell you more about it than I can. I was drunk all the time. Well, not exactly drunk just pissed. I got through a good few bags of weed as well. Jesus … not much else to do out there.

"Heh, Louis" Chrissy moaned to me one night in a blue-walled fly ridden hotel room in Wangabanga or Wooliwonga or someplace like that "When are you going to fuck me?"

I'd gone right off sex. I mean, I had too many other things on my mind. Every time Chrissy put her hand on my cock I managed to find some sort of excuse.

"I'm tired, Chris" was my favourite night one.

My favourite morning excuse was "I've got to get up. There's so much to do."

It worked for a while but Christine started taking it personally.

"You tired with me, Louis?"

The truth was I just wasn't interested any more. I'd been with Chrissy about eighteen months and the whole desire thing had worn off. I mean, when we'd first got together we went at it all the time. Then we slackened off and started fantasising about making it with other people. In Hawaii, Chrissy managed to sort that one out. After being disinterested in me for about three months, fucking that weirdo Sunshine made her all loving again. But the thing was ... I hadn't had a fling with anyone. I hadn't had a taste of strange. Know what I mean?

So there we were in Wangabanga and I just couldn't get any interest up for Chrissy. I mean I haven't talked about Chirstine's body yet. It's pretty good. She's no model, but she likes the old heave-ho. She's a mover, not one of those sorry souls who don't know what it's all about and who just take it however it comes. She turns on and knows what she likes. In fact, I'd go as far as to say that Chrissy is into a little kink ... enough to find something to do five nights a week. There's nothing more destroying to a love life than only getting it on every fourth Tuesday in the month. That sort of thing leads to a very cool and ordered relationship. It's the sort of stuff that makes heterosexual marriage a pathetic institution.

No. When I go through these disinterested periods they usually don't last longer than two weeks. In Wangabanga I was right in the middle of one. Chrissy was feeling insecure. She suspected that I'd had it off with Soochow Lu. Deep down I wished I'd had, but no, I'm one of those blokes who try to respect his friends. I mean, Jack was a good mate. I'd met him in Dar-es-

Salem and we'd got through a bottle of Johnny Walker together. Those sorts of friendships can never be broken. Gosh, if only I'd got Lu alone, I'd....

I was just getting to sleep in our fly-hole in Wangabanga when Chrissy had another go at violating me.

"I told you I was tired." I snarled.

"I can't put up with this any more" she shouted. "Either you fuck me or we're finished."

"I'm too tired!" I whimpered. I knew I was about to be interrogated.

"Jack wasn't too tired!" she said getting out of bed. She went to the bathroom.

Jack? What did he have to do with it? Jack? Chrissy returned from the bathroom with a glass of water. She threw it on me.

"What the hell are you doing?" I screamed sitting bolt up right.

"You're a fag" said Chrissy.

God, she could be a bitch at times. I mean, how do you answer something like that without starting on the defensive.

"I think you need to see a psychiatrist" I replied.

"Then we're both insane!" she answered.

Well, we'd reached a deadlock. Or so I thought.

"If you don't fuck me, Louis, I'll go back to Cairns and get Jack to do it for you again."

Jack? Again? Why, that no-good fucker. I'd been cuckolded again.

"You're such a sucker, Louis. You don't know when you're on to a good thing. Look at me" she said as she got astride me on the bed "Plenty of other men like what I've got. But you, you're such a fool! Look, I've got good tits ... and a wet cunt! What's the matter with me?"

She suddenly burst into tears and the situation was saved. She was once more full of remorse, this time for her indiscretion with Jack, and for the way she had just spoken to me. It was then for the first time that I realised the complete fullness of Christine's sexual nature. She had to be loved constantly or she became a frustrated and emotionally insecure individual. I had to recognise the fact that if I chose to ignore her sexual demands, she would seek out someone else to fulfil her wants.

All of a sudden, as quickly as my disinterested period had started, it went. Having sex with Chrissy became a matter of survival. From Wangabanga on, I made sure we made love every day.

TOMMY DIRTYNOSE

Smart snot Tommy Dirtynose was one of those kids with round-glasses who knew everything except how to wipe his own bum. His favourite book was the twenty volume Encyclopaedia Britannica. He was into 'heavy' reading and had no fear in declaring that comic books were "responsible for the de-education of romantics and the premature death of classicism."

No-one Tommy's own age knew what he

was talking about, and no one his senior ever listened to a word he said. Tasmania was one of those places at the end of the earth.

"All these trees here" ... he had a habit of talking to himself "and no-one turns the leaf of a book."

He was very astute, but thoughts like these made him very unhappy. It was his dream to escape into the world of Wittgenstein, Darwin, and Kant, and soon enough he would. Like all little Australian whizzes, he knew that his learning would take him to Sydney, to Paris, to London. Soon he would be able to forget the loneliness of being a genius surrounded by wilderness. Ahead lay a brilliant university career - lectureship, professorship, respect, and material comfort.

Yet, by a sheer twist of fate, he was to be undone. His Uncle Bruce, a man sea-tossed and wind-blown by life, sent young Tom a FEAR AND LOATHING book from Kathmandu for his sixteenth birthday. Between the covers of the Thompson book lay the mixed-up world that goes beyond naive childhood dreams.

Tom acquired some blue pills from a school-friend.

He was never the same again.

Nothing's new under the sun. We flew out of Perth for Nepal.

Nepal's one of those places you either love or hate. Most people love it. I've been to Nepal twice and think ... shit; I'll probably end up going there again. It's no

Shangri-la. Kathmandu can be a hellhole. That about sums it up.

I'd been warning Chrissy that I was about to start my own novel. I was surprised when she said that she was pleased that I had found something to put my energies into at last. She almost put me off.

Anyway, I started.

THE DEAD COW

It *all happened so fast.*

The cow was on the road and the truck hit a sharp blow on the hind-side. To the onlookers, the animal turned into a dead carcass blocking the two-lane highway that ran all the way to the capital.

Traffic backed up quickly in both directions as the cow's peasant owner and the truck driver haggled over compensation.

"A thousand rupees!!" the truck driver shouted to the assembled crowd "Tis outrageous!"

The ever-growing crowd of bus-drivers, truckers, motorcyclists, bike-riders, foot-travellers, itinerants, beggars, and field-peasants became the people's jury. They jostled with one another to lend their verdict. It was chaos.

The peasants were a ragged crew of docile semi-nomads made brainless by centuries of inter-breeding. Their tribal instinct over-road any sense of justice. They were quick to see that by a quirk of fate, a bony old milk less cow had suddenly been transformed into a thousand rupees.

"That's right!" an old wizened peasant goaded the thickset well-oiled truck-driver. "Doff up, or we'll get the police on to you for drinking and driving! I can smell Indian whisky on your breath."

The truck-driver noticeably wobbled. He tried to say something, but it came out as a stutter. "It's ... outrageous!" he stammered. "You're nothing but a bunch of toothless peasants. Look at this thing" he appealed to the crowd "it would barely have fetched a hundred rupees at a crooked market."

The crowd laughed.

In a further gush of self-redeeming pride, the truck-driver pleaded further with the crowd to side with him. But the crowd, which at first had been amused by the incident, then somewhat bored, were now anxious to get the dead animal off the road. Mumbles of advice began to seep out of the crowd.

"Pay up!"

"Give the old fool his money!"

"See what happens when you drink!"

"The police station's only five miles from here!"

"It's not worth it!"

"Give him the rupees and let's be on our way!"

Heeding the crowd, the truck-driver, a man of comparative wealth, dolefully commenced to peel ten one hundred rupee notes from a wad taken from his shirt pocket whilst a host of helpful men positioned themselves to move the cow to *the side of the road.*

Lo and behold! A miracle! The animal sprung to life. It stood up in the midst of the crowd with a vacant look that quickly turned to fright. Finally, coming to its senses, the poor beast still shocked and confused, mad a bolt for the safety of the nearest pasture.

The astonished crowd burst into whoops of delight. In the uproar, the old peasant who's animal had suddenly sprung to life again, snatched a hundred rupee note from the mesmerised truck-driver's hand, and set off in hot pursuit of his beast.

It had all happened so fast.

With the cow no longer blocking the highway, the traffic began to move as before, the memory of the incident marked only by a mile long tail of vehicles that the half-crazed peasants laughed out of sight.

It's time for me Christine to give you my opinion. I liked Louis's story, but it was obvious he had a long way to go if he wanted to be a novelist. Frankly, between you and me, Louis is better at fact than fiction. After all, I'm the writer, not Lou. He seems to have got it into his head that it's easy to write novels. He'll learn. And anyway, I've got a much better poem about a cow than that. Something I wrote on my twenty-first birthday.

DEAD BANANA FOR THE COWS

As the train begins to slow,
A sticky hand lets it go,

It hits the track all arms and legs
And lies prostrated in a manner
Unbecoming to the dead.

In a field heads are raised,
Blacks, browns, whites, and greys;
Some with horns, some without,
With rolling eyes and thoughts alike
They all prepare to fight.

Anyway, I should stick to my story.

The way it goes so far is that Tom Dirtynose has just swallowed some blue pills after reading a Hunter Thompson book sent to him by his uncle Bruce.

BRUCE

Bruce has only been in Nepal two weeks before his conscience started to bother him.

"Damn bed-bugs!" he cursed.

Perplexed, he trekked to Swayambu, the Monkey Temple, where he walked around in circles for hours turning the prayer wheels.

Dizzy, he rested on a hot wall at the top of the thousand steps that led back into the quagmire of everyday Nepalese life.

As he sat contemplating, a monkey threw a half-eaten mango at him that hit him in the goollies.

"Bloody little dwarfs!" he shouted in anger.

The monkeys started to chatter with laughter.

"I'll boomerang the lot of you!" he threatened.

In a rage, Bruce descended in a bow-

legged hobble the first flight of stairs in pursuit of the monkeys. They led him into the undergrowth.

"Oh that is a very crazy man," a peanut seller said to a pilgrim he was serving.

"I do not understand these foreigners" the pilgrim replied. "They are all madmen."

"Better to be mad than crazy" the peanut seller answered.

"I do not understand the difference" the pilgrim said derisively.

"Ah" said the vendor "Madmen are overtaken by excessive reasoning. Crazy fellows are overflowing with excessive emotions."

"And?" asked the pilgrim expecting a conclusion.

"I do not know," said the vendor "I know peanuts, and not what is in a man's heart or mind."

"Then you are a very crazy fellow" the pilgrim said with an uprightness.

"And you are a madman" said the peanut seller.

"How so!" said the pilgrim outraged?

"You have come up a thousand steps just to buy my peanuts," said the vendor. "That will be five rupees, please."

"What! Do you think I am a madman!" the pilgrim shouted. "Five rupees! You are crazy!"

"This we have already ascertained," said the peanut seller.

Meanwhile, the monkeys were lobbing mangoes at Bruce.

"Come down from those trees, you cowering bastards!" he wailed at them "I'll

have the lot of you!" he chattered. "I haven't come to Nepal to be made a monkey of!" he screamed jumping up and down.

The monkey's laughter shook the mango trees so much that the trees shed their fruit all at once and buried Bruce under a mango green mountain.

She could write all she wanted but I was away. I'd begun my novel. One thing I didn't want was Chrissy stealing my ideas. You know what it's like. One minute you're using the same toothbrush, and before you know it, all the bristles have fallen out.

That sort of stuff is bad news.

I still loved Christine but I was tired of being the one doing all the talking. It was her turn. All I wanted to do was concentrate on my fantasy. Ever since I'd left South Africa I'd wanted to voice my opinions about the rotten things that go on in that godforsaken place.

But what's the use.

When half way through April you've got a bunch of Yappies celebrating Adolph Hitler's birthday in a beer keller off Kotze Street, Hillbrow, you know that the bastards deserve everything that's coming to them.

I mean, when you walk into a bar and you're met by a seething mass of Afrikaners singing Nazi songs, you're stomach turns right over. The straight-arm salute and the 'Heil Seig' utterances are bad enough, but when half the fuckers are wearing swastika armbands, you know they're serious. Proud to call themselves Nazis, singing 'Happy Birthday Adolph' provokes such hysterical saluting and chanting, that it is soon noticed you're not joining in. Loads of blokes in South Africa run around with a gun in their vest and you're never quite sure when one's going to be pushed in your face. The general comradeship of the National Socialists is such a passionate conviction that if you're not with them, then, you're better dead. In South Africa the memory of Adolph Hitler is not one of hate. To the Afrikaners he's a god-sent hero.

No. I don't want to talk about South Africa.

Maybe I should just stick to talking about Christine after all. I could make a whole world out of her marriage. But I won't. It's crazy; I've been too many places to know where I belong. I'm confused.

Anyway, I'll pull myself together.

We were in Darjeeling, and I decided that I couldn't be a novelist like Chrissy because I just didn't have the patience. I found that I was better at telling short stories. We met a lot of other travellers, and it seemed that I was never short of a tale or two. I mean, some of the ones I told were right whoppers, but at least there was an element of truth in them. (I couldn't say that for Chrissy.)

I remember crossing the Darien Gap.

I trekked from Sanzurro along muddy tracks to climb over the jungle thick sierra towards Panama. My periodic raids on coco trees and my general slackness of pace led me to lose my way in the dense undergrowth. The subsequent tramp was at times an unbearable ardour in an almost dire situation as I struggled through wriggling creepers and slid innumerable times precariously down vertical slopes as the rotten vegetation yielded underfoot. But I persevered, taking little account of the accumulating cuts and gashes inflicted with searing pain on my arms and legs, and my face.

When I finally found a gully in which I half stumbled my way down the mountain, I waded through knee-deep pools of blackish water, and tore at the overhanging branches to make the stream a watery path leading towards the sea.

Emerging on a deserted coconut fringed beach - into a world of pleasure from sheer hell - I cut down some coconuts, tore off my clothes, and fell helplessly into the cradle of the waves. Joyously I floated on my back, eyes closed, aware only of the seas roar as she fought with the land. The pleasure of not existing, of being only another piece of debris waiting its turn to touch shore; the hypnosis of the endless pounding coupled with a blankness of mind that created a domain of peace within and without; the soothing softness of the sea offering its endless respite from the physical pain of the now forgotten jungle; all these things combined to make the sea a haven from the nastiness of the experience just undergone.

That reminds me. While I was in Darjeeling, I fell of a cliff. But that's another story, but Chrissy didn't want to hear it.

BEN

The chief monkey of the tribe was Ben.

Ben had seen many stranger things than mango mountains. In a winter so severe that the snow had descended right into the Kathmandu valley, Ben was returning to the slopes of Swayambu after making off with some goat's cheese from the shack of a hoarding merchant, when ... he ran into a snow yeti.

Yes, that's right ... a yeti snowman. It was ten feet tall and had a giant red banana as a nose.

At first Ben thought it was real. No. Even worse, his poor monkey brain computed that it was a Rakshasa, an evil spirit. No. At last he realised that it was the work of a bored-yeti.

Relieved, he dropped the cheese, and clambered up the snow yeti to steal the red banana. Suddenly to his horror, he saw a real yeti lumbering towards his pride and joy.

The yeti was carrying the skin of some animal that had been shaped into a hat for the snow yeti.

Ben, with a chatter and a gulp, disguised himself as a scarf by hanging around the neck of the snow yeti.

The yeti shuffled up in the snow.

"SNIFF ... SNIFF..." the yeti snuffed as he placed the hat on its creation. "SNIFF ... SNIFF..." the yeti's nose ran as he

straightened the snow yeti's nose. "SNIFF ... SNIFF..." the yeti reached to tighten the snow yeti's scarf. "SNIFF ... SNIFF..."

Pause.

The yeti nosed the air. "SNIFF ... SNIFF ... SNIFF ... "

With a final "SNIFFFFFFF..." the yeti looked, and saw the goat's cheese at his feet. He slowly bent to pick it up.

Ben took his chance. He seized the red banana and sprang onto the yeti's back and leaped off into the snow. With the banana in his teeth, he scurried for the trees.

The yeti, a slow-witted beast, neither felt nor saw Ben's departure. He ate the cheese, and from the trees, Ben saw him scratch his head and sniff around the snow yeti for the missing scarf and nose.

Ben chattered to himself and rushed on home to the Temple. He was thoroughly pleased with himself. The cheese would have been a nice winter nibble, but what better winter treat could a monkey have than a juicy red banana.

When I fell off the cliff in Darjeeling I was following a monkey path. It had suddenly narrowed and gone off to the right into a clump of bushes. Where monkeys fear to tread, I followed on, and before I knew it I was whizzing through fresh air.

The bushes were treetops.

It was one of those moments when your whole life flashes right in your face. Lucky it didn't completely obscure my vision or I would never have caught hold of the branch that stopped me from enjoying the rest of the hundred-foot drop.

Yip, there I was dangling with one arm from the limb of a skimpy Himalayan tree. In front of me was the cliff. Behind me, over my shoulder and twenty miles away was Katchenjunga, the third highest mountain in the world. Above me there was fresh air, below me there was fresh air. It was really all very pretty.

Chrissy had been about twenty yards behind me.

"Louis! Louis! Where are you?"

"Eh..." I said calmly "I wouldn't come this way if I was you."

"What ... why?"

"Why don't you go round another way" I said. I didn't want to alarm her. The second last thing I wanted was Chrissy at the top of the cliff in hysterics. The last thing I wished to see was her joining me. I mean, the branch just wouldn't have supported us both.

"I think it would be much better if you went the other way" I said again placidly.

"Okay, Louis."

By the time Chrissy came around the other side of the cliff, I was still half way up it.

"O my god!" I heard her exclaim in sheer panic. However, I'd made progress. I was no longer dangling from the branch; I was slowly climbing my way down the cliff. It was covered in creepers, and after a considerable number of heart-stopping leaps to safety; I reached the foot.

Chrissy was sitting on a rock. She never said a thing. She was in some sort of shock.

The incident taught me one thing. Never follow monkey paths. For you never know when the path is going to take to the trees.

"Are you all right, Chris?" I asked.

She nodded.

"Well" I said, "I suppose we better push on if we want to get to Sikkim."

She agreed.

And so we did. We never talked about the incident until we got to Calcutta. I suppose in retrospect, I had cheated death. Yet again, I've always led a charmed sort of life.

RED NANA

Red Nana had belonged to a bunch at one time. He had been a native of Kaniyakumari, and had with his relatives and friends been exported. Shipped by boat to Bombay, train to Delhi, truck to Kathmandu, he had passed by cart, stall, and basket into rural Nepal. How he had come into the possession of the yeti is very hard to say, but Red Nana had felt very out of place in the snow. He longed to return to the heat of Tamil Nadu.

But it was not to be.

Red Nana, thick skinned though he was ... sadly was for the eating. Ben, the cheeky temple monkey, cruelly peeled back Nana's skin. Red's naked flesh lay exposed to Ben's pink tongue and yellow teeth. Red knew the end had come. A vision came to him. A vision of it's ancestral home in far Ecuador. A vision of the flight from Ecuador and a short stay on a British plantation on

the slopes of Kilimanjaro, then the final
transportation journey to India. In a flash it
came to him all. The sights and pains of
migrating across the high seas: the Pacific
to the Atlantic; the Atlantic to the Indian;
the sub-tropics to the high Himalayas. It
was such a traumatic vision that Nana felt
immediately depressed. He was nearing
death. He was dying alone in a foreign land
far from any of his own kind. He began to
weep, and shiver, and moan ... and Ben,
bewildered and uncertain what to do,
dropped Nana on the forest floor.

Suddenly, Garuda the temple eagle
appeared as if from nowhere. He snatched
Red Nana from the cold hard forest floor
and carried him off. Sweeping to the tops,
Garuda soared upwards towards Swarga
until he was barely a pinpoint in the sky.
Then ... BLIP! He was gone.

> Eagle in the light blue sky
> Soaring with your eagle eye,
> Banana in your hungry jaw,
> Fly, fly, fly.

Sometimes Christine's writing makes
me want to throw up out the window. It can
be so pathetically facile. I mean, none of it
is real, there's no real adventure. She's led
such a sheltered life that she doesn't write
from experience. By contrast, my charmed
life once took me eighty miles across a
desert in Africa. I was escaping the green-
monkey disease that had broken out in the
Sudan. Defying quarantine and house
arrest, I set off across the Sahel with an

English companion and a Japanese itinerant.

Wait a minute, here. This is my story too, I want to say something about Louis. Every hotel we stayed in on our trip around the world was a hellhole fleapit. You see, Louis likes to suffer, he's not happy unless he's penniless and homeless. He's the most generous person in the world; he'll give away his last cent to a rich man, but only because he enjoys being broke. You see, the thing is, Louis can't stand responsibility.

That's the crunch.

He didn't realise when he talked me into going on this hair-brained penniless sojourn around the globe that I'd be his biggest headache. After all, I do openly admit that my previous travelling was bucket-shop type stuff and that I wasn't prepared for the squalor of Mexico and the feudalism of Kathmandu. I am of a gentler nature than Louis, the rough tough man of endless exploits and continents. I'm feminine, I'm sensitive, and I'm Scorpio. Louis is sexist, thick-skinned, and Aries. He doesn't seem to understand that Arians do not rule the world.

GARUDA

Garuda the eagle was a lonely old bird whose mate had died five years before from natural causes. He spent most of his time dozing in his eyrie waiting for something different to happen. Eating Nana in mid-winter was an unusual experience.

Garuda was quite a wise old crack. He

had six surviving eaglets living in the Kathmandu Valley. But things had been so quiet in the Valley, the vultures hadn't left the comfort of the city for years.

Therefore it was a welcome surprise when he saw a Bangladeshi Airways jet crash into one of the mountains ringing the Valley. He was immediately aroused, and off he went to investigate. When he arrived at the site of the devastation, Garuda was awed by the size of the big metal bird that dwarfed him. However, it was fun to see silly flying-men dead, injured, or scattered helplessly on the mountains. It somehow restored Garuda's faith in his belief that all beings were equal in luck and fate, and that man-made things were not built to last.

He swooped down, and perching himself on a rock.

He curiously watched a woman in a Tahitian batik dress die.

Death. What a cheery lovely subject for Chrissy to contemplate.

Look, I'll let you into a secret. This story, my story, Chrissy's story, it has all gone a bit adrift. I mean, sure, I could quite easily talk on and on about me; how wonderful my life has been up 'til now, but hell, do you really want to know? For instance, do you really believe all this crap about India and stuff? You know, falling off cliffs, getting stuck in deserts? I mean, wouldn't you be happier hearing about my lovely innocent childhood instead.

Like everyone else, the first thing I ever wrote was my name.

LOUIS
I had begun.

How long ago those weary short-trouser days seem now ... cat ... dog ... kick ... girl. Long summer days of footballs half my size, and bullies twice my age, who wrote on my school-bag

WANKER

Those kind of things made an impression on my infant brain trying to cope with words like ... pussy ... bitch ... fag ... you know, all those sort of things overheard on street corners and scrawled on park benches.

FUCK THE POPE

What did it all mean? Walls painted white, then painted black to erase all the daubs of green paint and yellow emulsion which formed vague sentences like ...

FENIAN RULE
PRODDY BASTARD

Religious differences that I was soon made to feel by never being allowed to wear green ... never being allowed out wearing orange. Eventually it was explained to me in terms of IRA ... Celtic ... Ireland ... Mother Mary ... 1690 ... 1707 ... 1846 ... 1916 ... and a whole load of other dates and figures and names I had to remember, like ... Boyne ... Enniskillen ... Derry ... that I was told was Over the Water which as far as I was concerned could have been in

Australia, or California, or Mecca that for us was Ibrox and Hampden and Wee Pollok ... where on good days at home games, when the ball sailed over heads and into the River Cart. It was sixpence and a dry towel if you fetched it out ... you got to see your own name in the club ledger.

> LOUIS STEWART........... BALLBOY
> Fetched bladder from burn 6d

And that night the Evening Times reporter, a man with a red nose and a beer gut and a forest of red beard ... would write in the pink edition –

> Pollok were saved in time and in
> usual fashion when the ball was
> kicked over their goal by Bailleston
> who were in a desperate panic to
> play for time. But for the quick
> recovery of the ball from the Cart
> by wee Louis Stewart, which caught
> Bailleston with only nine men on
> the field, Pollok surely would not
> have scored their winning goal,
> and would not have gone through
> to the final of the Scottish Junior
> Cup without a replay.

I admired the style of that journalist ... he had a quick eye for even the smallest hero. Me dad cut out the article and said

"Louis, you'll be famous yet."

Loius wasn't my real name, but my dad had changed it by deed poll when I was two years old. It was the name of kings.

"It was for your own good, son. We made a big mistake when you were born.

Named you after the actor Jimmy Stewart. There are far too many Jimmy's in this part of the world."

He was right. I never liked being called James. In my class at school there was ... Jimmy MacDonald, Jimmy MacPherson, Jim Anderson, Jimmie MacGregor, Jimmy Robertson, aye, and even a Jimmy Smith! In our class of thirty-six, if you included me, there were twenty-nine of us not called Jimmy. But even worse, there were eight Mary's; Brown, Beaton, Seaton, Carmichael, MacIntosh, Morrison, Houston and Hamilton. It was tedious listening to the teacher calling out the register but at least the sound of my name made the walls sing.

"LOUIS STEWART!"

And teacher MacTavish would always stop and say

"Such a fine name ... a royal one at that ... contaminated by such a rudimentary modern enigma like you that typifies rebellion in junior secondary schools. It is quite beyond me."

"Don't you like me, Miss?"

"Do you mean the name ... or you?"

"The name, Miss?"

"Some of us have to live with our parent's eccentricities, boy."

"But, Miss..."

"Sit down, master Stewart."

"My dad says..."

"Sit down, Stewart!"

"But my dad says ....!"

"Sit down! You will write out..."

And that's what I had to do, write out

MY NAME IS LOUIS STEWART, AND I MUST NOT SPEAK LIKE A PRATT.

One hundred times.

It didn't have much effect. If nothing else it gave me good writing practice.

Louis liked to dwell on the past. In my own way I loved Louis. He wasn't a cruel man. In fact, in some ways Lou was too soft. He was so easy going, too easy going. I think he gave me too much personal freedom. I'm not saying that too much personal freedom is a bad thing, but sometimes it can leave the door wide open for bad things to come into your life. Sticking with one person might keep you to the straight and narrow, and god's teeth, we all know how boring that can be. However, getting into polygamous relationships leads to all sorts of, well, bad things. When I had that fling with Sunshine at Kokee it was great at the time. But it sure shook up Louis. On top of that, I got pregnant. Lucky enough, I read the signs and knew right away the state I was in. I had one of those quick-in quick-out vacuum jobs.

I never told Louis, it was one of those secrets that I had to keep to myself. Sure, I could talk to other women about it, but not Louis. Up until I had screwed Sunshine, Louis had always seemed pretty secure about our relationship. He was so sure he took it for granted.

I guess it must have come as a shock to him to find out that I wasn't the Miss Little Innocent he thought I was. After all, I had been married, and there was no way I was ever going to give up my personal happiness for any man. If I want to do something, I do it.

The time I had with Jack while Louis was trying to seduce Soochow Lou was partially a counter-action to Louis's behaviour. I did like Jack, though. I could talk to him about a lot of things that Louis just didn't understand. He was sensitive. Living with the Chinese had taken a lot of the chauvinistic Western male out of him. I couldn't live with Jack, there were a lot of things in his character that I found irritating, but he was a very nice lover.

If there is one thing I've learned about men, then, it's the fact that they are all sexists. They can't help themselves. Men are men even with their balls cut off. As men go, Louis is not that bad. He has his Bolshie moments, but he forgives and forgets quickly. I wish I could say that he was the love of my life, but I think I don't believe in any of that sort of crap any more.

THE BATIK SKIRT

The Batik Skirt hated being exposed on a Himalayan mountain.

She was homesick for Tahiti ... or Fiji ... or even Singapore where she had added spice to boutique shop collections.

She had been bought, worn and then packed away in a tiny travel bag by her new mistress, a slim exotic French 'freak' with very beautiful legs. Together, they travelled up the Malay Peninsula ... Penang,

Koh Samui and Bangkok. They spent a week in Burma, the Batik Skirt having a delightful time in Mandalay. They flew on to Dacca where the Skirt became incredibly jaded from being stared at by the Bangla people. Everywhere the Skirt went, children, mothers, fathers, then men ... until finally entire northern villages would follow her up the street and touch her to see if she were real.

As they boarded the Bihman Airways plane that would take them on to Nepal, she looked forward to the companionship of her mistress in Kathmandu. In flight she dreamed of seeing the Living Goddess.

But tragedy struck.

Now, to find herself a casualty midst a scene of human horror, she started to stiffen in the icy mountain waste as the snow began to cover up her bright vibrant colour.

More fantasy from Chrissy. I think my social realism is better.

MARY BEATON ... MARY SEATON
MARY CARMICHAEL ... and I.

This is what Mary Hamilton sang as the lassies skipped in the playground. My mammy told me it was an old song about the four women who had attended Mary, Queen of Scots, at Linlithgow Palace. My pals were into a different type of skipping ... doggin'.

Doggin' was a dunce's game. I only did it when the hot summer weather came around ... the boilers of the main-line Royal Scot express burnt all the way from Glasgow Central to Euston London. Most times my pals got belted for doggin' school and running wild on the golf courses or swinging from ropes strung from the branches of an elm or a willow or a chestnut tree growing by the banks of the burn. And it was always the Jimmies ... Jimmy MacDonald or Jimmy MacPherson or Jimmy Robertson that landed back first ... or headfirst in the Cart.

But they didnae care ... they pretended they were pirates and swam to the bank and stripped off their school clothes, dried them on the branches of an elder or a rowan or a hawthorn then sat down and talked about blackbirds and thrushes and cuckoos and moor-hens and about other poor creatures and about stickle-backs and baggie-minnows and tadpoles and about the catfish that swam up the Clyde and up the length of the Cart through Whitecraigs and Pollok and Pollok Estate before reaching Pollokshaws where they turned round and swam back through the Estate and Pollok and Whitecraigs to emerge opposite Clydebank and John Brown's Shipyard where they built the Queen Mary and the Queen Elizabeth and the Queen Elizabeth the Second and if it wasn't for the Cart they would never have been launched and turned round in the river to sail off to foreign places.

Aye such were the hot summer days when my pals needed letters, excuse notes, scribblings from Mammies about doctors and dentists and bilious fevers and retching which I would write for tuppence that would never work and Jimmy MacDonald would get belted and I would get belted for trying to subvert the course of Scottish school-justice and we'd be placed at the front of the class and she'd call me STEWART! ... or LOUIS STEWART! ... and never LOUIS.

On days like that my eyes would wander to the window and the Royal Scot would go past and the puffy white clouds rolling across the summer sky, until LOUIS STEWART! from MacTavish brought me back to class work and the staring chalked black-board which read –

WHAT IS THE CAPITAL OF BECHUANALAND

that was somewhere in Africa where Livingston had gone after leaving Scotland which none of us doubted existed or even protested as being British or questioned that it should be any other colour on the map but pink or that it was three times larger than the U.K. and twelve times larger than Scotland and that the answer was -

"Well? Louis Stewart?"

"I don't know, Miss."

that made her write on the board

THE CAPITAL OF BECHUANALAND IS MAFEKING

- that I had then to write twenty times.

Louis and I smoked a lot of drugs during our travels but it didn't seem to get him to be less realistic in his tale telling. We were staying in a cockroach Calcutta hotel on Sutter Street, and I was out of my brains, when Louis came back from the post-office with a letter from Alice. I was so enfeebled by opium; I hadn't the strength to open it.

The letter lay by my bed all of that day and the next until Louis insisted that I open it.

So three weeks after the letter was sent, and two days after I'd received it, I slit it open with my opium knife and read

> Dear Chrissy,
> Enclosed is a letter from your agent. It looked so important; I thought I'd send it on to you. I'm sorry you stopped writing every day. It was really fascinating. I don't know what happened to you after Hawaii, but I imagine it is far too exciting to write about.
> I do hope this letter catches you in Calcutta. I look forward to you coming back sometime. A year is a long time, and I sometimes think that you won't ever want to come back to dull old England. Life here is pretty boring. I still haven't got a job, but I'm in three choirs so that gives me something to do.
> Please give Louis my love.
> I miss you,
> love ALICE

Reading Alice's letter exhausted me. I was too feeble to open the enclosed letter from my agent. I was actually frightened. I had given up on him, and no doubt, he had given up with me. I had written him a letter from Mexico telling him to go and stuff himself, but I hadn't posted it.

The letter lay by my bed all of that day and the next two until Louis, short of patience said

"For fuck's sake, Chris, get it together. I think it's time you got off the opium."

I entirely agreed, but that was easier said than done. Opium was legal in Calcutta. There was this little government shop on Beni-something Street where I could buy a tola of black opium for sixteen rupees. It was costing me less than 10p a gram, and naturally, there was as much there as I wanted. Louis didn't get into it as much as I did which was maybe just as well, for without Louis, I might have had a hard time getting out of Calcutta.

The letter from my agent still lay unopened. Furious at my lethargy, Louis threw it at me, and ordered me to open it.

"Don't tell me what to do," I screeched from my opium craze. But I opened the letter.

DEAR MISS KEEMUN,

WE ARE GLAD TO INFORM YOU THAT WE HAVE FOUND A PUBLISHER FOR YOUR NOVEL THE CARDBOARD COWGIRL. WE WOULD BE MOST GRATEFUL IF YOU COULD CONTACT US IN THE NEAR FUTURE IN ORDER THAT WE MIGHT DISCUSS THE TERMS OF CONTRACT.

I couldn't have been at lower ebb when this news arrived. For when I look back on it, I realise that I had the Calcutta-Opium-Bengal-Bubble-Blues.

Down in the gutter in Calcutta
With the waste, the sewage, and trash,
with the commotion of rickshaws and taxis,

trams, and buses jam packed;
I was smoking a chillum and watching
from behind an opium haze -
A seething mass of faceless souls
and the plots of a thousand plays.

I had to escape, find somewhere to hide.

THE SNOW

The poor Snow. It was hard for it to cover up the gaiety of the batik dress. It had lifted and rolled itself across the grey Himalayas to come to this. It felt that it would rather have fallen as rain.

"This is buggery" it told itself "Once I've lain, then there is no chance of travel. If I were a raindrop, I could have fallen on a slope that drained into the Ganges or the Bramaputra. I would have found myself in the Bay of Bengal. I would have been well-companioned and ready to bob the Seven Seas."

You see, there were islands in the world that the Snow never had the slightest chance of visiting. Lovely tropical islands. But the Snow, in its cool white form, just didn't get the chance. Ill-luck had caught it up with a cold Wind blowing in from Shangri-La.

Shangri-la. That's Chrissy all over, looking for some paradise. I know better from my travels. When I went to Bechuanaland, somebody had got around to calling the place Botswana. I'd come a long way from MacTavish's schoolroom. I was travelling through the Kalahari in a kombi-van with a German couple. It was the bad old days when the Americans were keeping Smith's Rhodesia going. The dumper-cars of Rhodesian chrome destined for the industries of America, were parked on a Francistown side-line awaiting a White-House decision whether to stop the chrome trade or not. You see, the Americans were on this humanitarian-lets-get-the-world-to-love-us kick which was wearing thin in Washington. As usual the American paranoia had set in and the Americans had reverted to their belief that the world had never loved Americans and that they never would.

When I got to Francistown, the boxcars had started to roll. The main street was deserted and me and my companions, Pete and Urena, were as parched as white chalk after five hundred miles of bush land. All the stores were closed, but the mile long train of moving boxcars that blocked the main street made them turn down a side alley. As luck would have it, we emerged opposite the railway station, a string of stores, and a couple of take-aways.

We parked the kombi and got out.

Everyone stared. There was nothing but black faces and fingers pointing in our direction. A couple of blacks went up to the kombi and wiped the dust of the battered orange number-plate to reveal ... SWA B752.

We shrugged the incident off and entered a store. Buying cokes, I leant against a hitching post in the store doorway trying to catch someone's eye. But there was something strange going on. There was an odious sense of distrust. Everyone looked the other way.

I let my vision wander further a field. I noticed that every piece of rolling stock in the railway yard had the black and silver lettering of Rhodesia Railways. The Botswana railway line was Rhodesia's only link to a port. Cape Town.

Suddenly a black policeman brought me to my senses.

"Are you the driver of that van?" he rasped.

"Eh?" I responded rather slowly.

"Are you the driver of that van?" he rasped again.

"No" I replied.

Before I could say anything that would clarify the situation, the policeman ran off at a trot. Within two minutes, he returned with a sergeant and two other officers.

"Are you the driver of that Kombi?" the sergeant asked.

"No" I replied again as Urena came and stood by me.

"Are you the driver?" the sergeant asked Urena.

"No" she said.

"Well! Who is?" the sergeant demanded to know.

Urena and I pointed to Pete who was busy with the store owner changing Dmarks into Pula.

"Have you just driven from South West Africa?" the sergeant asked bluntly.

"No" said Pete with a smile.

"Why then have you South West

plates?" the sergeant inquired suspiciously.

"They're not South West plates" Louis interceded.

"They're German" Urena added.

"It says S.W.A.," the sergeant continued.

"Ha..." said Pete "That is an abbreviation for the town we come from in Germany."

"Schwartzenbach" said Urena.

"Schwirt...sen?" the sergeant said confused. Great whirlpools went round and round in his eyes. Then a light shone.

"Okay, okay! You'll have to come with us to the police station."

"For what?" asked Urena.

"For questioning!" said the sergeant.

"Why?" I asked.

"Don't ask me why" the sergeant bellowed. His eyes went into whirlpools again then cleared. "Just do what I tell you" he added "And remember, don't try anything. We'll be following you."

I felt my sides ready to burst with laughter.

"Follow us he says," said Urena as she got in the kombi.

"We don't even know where the police station is!" said Pete.

The policemen, six of them now, clambered into their pick-up. As the sergeant reversed the pick-up, he backed into a car. As he pulled away, the bumper of the car was wrenched off. It had become snagged on the pick-up's tow bar. Two of the policemen leapt out and disengaged the bumper from the pick-up. They left it lying in the middle of the dusty street.

They led the way to the police station by sitting on the kombi's tail and shouting directions to Pete from behind. They weren't all that smart.

Arriving at the police station, they were shuffled into the Inspector's room. The Inspector, bleary-eyed and reeking of booze, proceeded to interrogate us.

"Are you mercenaries?" he asked.

"O!" said Urena

"Good god!" said Louis.

"No!" said Pete.

"But you've just come from Rhodesia" the Inspector said in a loud tone.

"No we haven't" I said.

"We've just come from Zambia," said Pete.

"Then why do you have a South West registration plate?" the Inspector grinned.

"It's German!" said Urena.

"But now you are on your way to Rhodesia?" the Inspector stated.

"No" said Louis.

"South Africa" said Pete.

"So you have come from Rhodesia!" the Inspector shouted triumphantly.

"No" said Louis.

"We've told you" said Urena.

"Zambia" said Pete.

"Are you sure you are telling the truth?" asked the Inspector.

"Yes!" we all shouted.

"Then you are not mercenaries?" the Inspector said.

"No!" we shouted again.

The Inspector seemed disappointed that

we were not mercenaries.

"I have only four hundred and twenty eight men left" the Inspector cried. "How can I take on the Rhodesian Army with a handful of ill-equipped men who know how to hold a bottle better than a rifle."

Louis looked about the room at the sorry bunch of policemen in attendance.

"Yesterday" the Inspector went on "the Rhodesians kidnapped two of our people. We chased them to the border. They played hide-and-seek with us. Shot one of my men." The Inspector went all-sad. Suddenly, he became angry. "If any white Rhodesians or mercenaries come this way, we'll lock them up for good!"

Satisfied that they weren't mercenaries, the Inspector let me and my two friends go.

Just in case someone took a pot shot at us, we drove out of Francistown as fast as the speed limit would allow.

By the time Louis and I got out of Calcutta and down the coast to Puri, Louis had got foul with malaria. He'd had it before, so it was ten times worse than it should have been. For three days he was in a fever and I really thought he was going to die. I prayed so hard to every god in India ... it took all the skin off my knees.

But it was worth it. Louis was saved!

He was in a fever for three more days, but he slowly came round. After six days, he was able to get out of bed. I took him down to the beach in the early morning and we sat and watched the Indian Ocean break in. I was so relieved that he was alive. He had lost so much weight that I could see almost every bone in his body. His skin was ashen, and it took some time for him to get some colour back.

He was very quiet. He had talked quite a lot while he was in fever, a lot of gibberish nonsense, and for a while his brain wasn't quite right. But his determination to live was second to none. I'll say one thing for Louis. When the bad cards are dealt, he demands a new hand. It is not a perfect analogy, but it sums Louis up quite well.

As for the malaria ... it was six days of total blank for Louis, and a hundred and forty-four hours of sheer hell for me.

THE WIND IN THE RIGGING

The Wind was more fortunate. It continued right down into the Indian Ocean where it got caught up in the sails of a Chinese junk. It whispered and tickled the canvas in playful jest. But the sails weren't amused, and as soon as they found their chance, they took it.

They captured the wind in their riggings.

The Wind struggled. It didn't like being trapped and put to use like a slave. It gathered and brooded its strength, and in no time, the junk was surrounded by a ferocious typhoon.

The captain of the junk ordered the sails to let go of the Wind.

"If not" he cried, "We are doomed!"

But the stupid sails, ignorant of the

Wind's might, refused to give up their hostage.

The captain ordered the masts to be hewn and cast overboard. But before the tasked was completed, the Wind ripped the sails from the rigging and carried them off into the vortex of the storm.

The junk was spun adrift as the Wind pursued the sails to complete its revenge.

My malaria was over. I've had other hairy times. Bigotry and racism are at the root of a lot of it. I mean, California was no different from Botswana. I've been to California a few times; I've even been a past resident of the state. Believe me, mate, the colour of your skin in that fine Republican paradise makes all the difference. Yet somehow, even the Caucasians find it hard to get along with one another. There's no such chance of someone being just a plain old Californian. Nope. Everybody's got to be Irish, or Polish, or Portuguese.

It just so happened that where I settled down in California for a year was a Portuguese town. It had been there since the first settlers had landed in northern California way back in 1602 or whenever. I found time to write it down in Calcutta. I left myself in the story.

They were putting in the irrigation system of a new Hayward park, and all day long, Manuel, a little Portuguese labourer ordered Scottish Louie about with a superior attitude. He also looked into the business of the Japanese plumber, giving free advice that slowly maddened the plumber. In a fit of despair, Scottish Louie and Dave the plumber broke early for lunch to escape their Portuguese tormentor. They left him to his lunch, on the hill beneath a eucalyptus, to chew the view.

Dave and Louie were away an hour. When they returned they felt rested and ready to start again despite the ninety-degree heat. Over lunch they had decided that they had to badger Manuel into minding his own business so that they could get on with their own work. In the morning nothing had been accomplished as Manuel had wasted their time by trying to drive a way through the baked hard earth beneath a concrete walkway.

Somehow, a nine-foot long hole had to be made from one side of the walkway to the other so that a sprinkler pipe could be laid beneath it. To conform to safety regulations, the pipe had to be eighteen inches beneath the concrete. Manuel had tried several times to hammer-drive a metal pole through one side and out the other. To no avail, he tried from both sides with the hope that they would meet in the middle. Dave and Louie tried to reason with Manuel that one pointed up and the other pointed down and that they would miss by two feet. But Manuel wouldn't listen. He was determined to do it his way, and went at it with such fervour that he hammered one of the pipes so deep into the earth that it wouldn't come out again.

Dave and Louie raised their eyebrows

and sighed when Manuel said he would drive his truck in, wrap a chain around the pipe, and haul it out with his vehicle. He ordered Louie to cut down a twelve-foot tree so that his wheels would have something to grip, but Louie refused. He liked trees and saw no sense in hacking down one of the few trees in the new park. Of like mind, Dave walked away in disbelief at the turn of events.

Manuel spent twenty minutes cutting down the tree while Dave and Louie worked on something else. Then suddenly both spun around to see Manuel's truck, wheels spinning, hurdling the trunk of the tree and getting stuck in the loose dirt banked-up along the length of the ditch. Manuel's wheels spun and spun until Dave told the Portuguese madman to step down. With Dave at the wheel, Louie on the tailgate to weigh the back wheels, Dave edged the truck out of the rut. He shouted to Manuel to connect the chain to the pipe, but the chain came flying off in their faces when Dave shot the truck forward. Backing up once again and reconnecting the chain, they managed after a few long pulls to whip the pipe out of the hole.

Half an hour later, Manuel had the same pipe stuck in the same hole again. This confirmed Dave and Louie's suspicions, something they'd been talking over during lunch. It was obvious that Manuel had no brains.

About this time the City Inspector of Works showed up to see how the work on the park was progressing. She saw the *three workers standing by the concrete walkway. They were arguing. Finding out what was going on, she suggested that they take a break and start on the other three walkways that had to be undermined. As Manuel started to complain, Louie got on with the job and started driving through the earth with pipe and sledgehammer. Tired, he stopped, and Manuel relieved him and drove the pipe through to the other side. Everyone gave out a big whoop of delight.*

As they started on the next one, Manuel sarcastically started calling Louie Boss and Sir and Yes Boss, and No Sir, just like the hateful South African blacks spit at their Yappy masters.

The tension rose. It was one of the hottest afternoons of the summer. They poured sweat. The urban smog hung over San Francisco Bay as Louie lined-up the pipe for the drive through to the other side of the next walkway. Manuel huffed and puffed that it couldn't be done. Louie would be driving through solid rock. Yet, in a matter of minutes he was through.

Louie in a moment of triumph said to Manuel

"See what happens when you let me be Boss!"

Manuel, a proud little man, attempted to hide his anger. He tried to turn the situation around. He jumped out of the ditch, and said

"Yes, you Boss now. Yes Sir, you big Boss now. You big Boss!" and threw his arms around Louie. He continued to chant "You Boss now! You Boss now."

Louie threw him off. Manuel stood grinning, but Louie had a reply.

"Yes. You should have let me be Boss ages ago. Everyone in Europe knows that the Portuguese don't have any brains."

Manuel's mouth opened wide in disbelief. Dave, who had been watching from the side, almost fell on the ground in laughter. He knew Louie was joking and saw the desired effect his words had had on Manuel. It kind of sobered Manuel up.

"I like evryone" answered Manuel "It no matter if blanco, black, or brown, evryone mismo. I like evryone."

"I like everyone too" said Louie "but I can't work with everyone."

No more was said. Manuel straightened up his act and put his back into the remaining walkway. The City Inspector helped him while Dave went back to his pipe laying and Louie to a ditch twenty yards away.

By the end of the day, Manuel and Louie had ascended to a mutual respect that enabled them to swap life-stories. It had been a hot day, and it was over. They were all a day older, and neither held a grudge.

When Louie turned up at the park the following morning, Tony de Silva, his Portuguese boss paid him off. At first Louie didn't understand. He didn't ask any questions, it had been temporary work, and anyway, with the heat he'd rather lay by the pool than dig ditches.

That evening, Japanese Dave called by his apartment to tell him that the Race Relations people had descended on the park *later that morning with accusations of discrimination against Portuguese. They threatened to take the contract away from the Portuguese sub-contractor. They had been looking for Louie, as according to the City Inspector, who as it turned out was also of Portuguese descent, Manuel had been discriminated against. The City Inspector had told her Portuguese City Engineer boss about their little incident at the new park. The City Engineer had rounded up a Portuguese hit-team to put a little god-fearing civility into the Scotsman.*

Fortunately, Louie had gone home. Dave said that they were all crazy and that it was a Portuguese mafia that ran Hayward. They couldn't fire him because everyone in California knew that the Japanese had been the most discriminated against during the forties. Californians were still expurgating their guilt for the way they had treated Japanese Americans. As for Louie, well, he was only a Scotsman, and everyone knew that Scottish Americans ran the Treasury, the Free Masons, and every third President. Running a Wasp out of their Portuguese town was the least they could do.

Louie, Louie, Louie. He always had to be at the centre of his stories. He could never put himself aside and make up exciting characters. All of his had to be real.

THE JUNK

The junk was washed up on the beaches

of Diego Garcia. Noluck Jim, the Chinese captain, was escorted first to the brig then hence to the commander of the NATO naval Base.

"Admit it, Noluck Jim. You're a spy, aren't you?"

It was a tough interrogation, but Noluck Jim kept his cool.

"Ah so ... no speak Inlish so well. But beg pardon. This boy very good Blitish subject."

"Hong Kong man, commander" a smart junior officer informed his superior.

"Yo ... Hong Kong ... but no Kowloon" said Noluck Jim.

"I like Aberdeen best myself" said the commander. "Maybe you should have stayed in harbour, Sunny Jim."

Maybe so, chief" replied Noluck Jim.

The commander beckoned to the smart junior officer who had spoken up before. He whispered in his ear.

"He was carrying tea, sir."

"Is that all?" the commander said in disbelief.

"We found some crates of Scotch. I thought..."

"You thought what, lad?"

"Nothing, sir." The officer was cursing himself for letting the information slip out.

"Right" said the commander "How many crates are there?"

"Well..."

"Come along, lad. Spit it out."

"About three hundred, sir."

"Black Johnnie" said Noluck Jim.

The commander's eyes lit up. "Right" he

said "Buy the whole lot off him, number one."

"Yes, sir."

"And put Sunny Jim and his crew on a flight for the mainland."

"Hong Kong?"

"Anywhere. Colombo. Singapore. Let him find his own way home."

"Aye aye, sir!"

Noluck Jim was removed from the presence of the commander.

"Anything else, sir?" the junior officer asked.

"A triple whiskey on the double, lad."

"O yes, sir ... there was one other thing.

"Yes?

"The tea-chests, sir."

"Tea-chests?"

"The ones washed ashore when the junk went down. That's what the whiskey's in, sir."

"Hold on to them, lad. I've a niece who keeps all her writings in one. They can be jolly useful."

I don't have much time any more to talk about Chrissy. I used to talk about her all the time, but after she got that letter from her agent, it was the start of the end for us. It was becoming obvious to both us that we weren't really compatible. I mean, we loved each other in our own peculiar ways, but we just didn't have it in us to spent the rest of our lives together. And anyway, who has? The letter from her agent finally confirmed that we were on our way home. I knew Chrissy was getting homesick, and that all those drugs in India were just an escape from the disorientating melee of Hindu life.

To be honest, I was getting homesick too. I was beginning to miss Radio One and all the music media crap which we all know is junk if we get too much of it. Out in India I was getting nothing. Chrissy was always too stoned to fuck. By the time she got off the drugs it was April and too friggin' hot to go near each other. Not that sex was that important, we've been through that one already. But all along, it was sex that had been the greatest bond in our relationship.

Of course, the spiritual wash we went through in India was amazing. We went into India with our spiritual consciousness as dirty as sin could get. I don't know what colour sin is supposed to be, but I must admit, we were pretty damn black. We had a lot of red in us, a bit of blue, loads of green, and the occasional smear of brown. By the time we were ready to leave India, we'd been to about two hundred temples and shrines. We were completely bleached. We emerged from the Taj Mahal lily white. We had been through the Twenty-Two trials.

THE TWENTY-TWO TRIALS OF A TRAVELLER

> *He has lived the life of a wanderer,*
> *and much has he conquered and borne,*
> *he's lived with the twenty-two troubles*
> *in order to learn and to know*
>
> *that though weakened and ravished by*
> *hunger,*

and covered in rivers of veins,
he'd take only his rationed measure
and wander on cheerful and sane.

Oh enough of this, Louie! There is enough wind in the world to blow all memories away. A storm in Mahablipuram washed way the he following letters and essays we had written.

COMMANDER FREDDY by Christine
A FATE IN PARADISE by Louis
BLUE LIGHTS by Christine
A LETTER from Larry
NEVER BE TIRED BY CHANGE by Louis

Luckily my novel remained intact and I did recover one of my sodden essay papers that had stuck to a ratha instead of being washed into the sea.

BLUEY

The mushroom, the one that did Freddy in, had come from Oregon. She was quite a big tess as far as mushrooms go. Her leg was kind of spindly, but her head had an enormous bump on it. The bump looked just like a nipple.

Unfortunately, that nipple was Bluey's downfall. A piece of bad ecological chemistry made her easy picking for the long-haired homesteaders whose field she grew in.

It had been a nice life really. While she had been a spoor, Bluey had lived in a nice comfortable cowpat with the rest of her family. A pig had treaded on Mom and Da, but it had all been quite painless.

SQUASH!!

After that, the family had taken care of itself. They'd sprouted during an extremely dry spell and had been saved from shrivelling by some cow piss. When the weather finally broke, the rain was so heavy, Bluey managed to grow four inches across.

It was a glorious few days that was eventually spoiled by a red-face homesteader. As soon as he set his beady bloodshot eye on her ... it was OOUF!

Thus unceremoniously picked, Bluey was laid out on a tray with her brothers and sisters. She soon turned grey, and thus ill and ashen, she was shipped East in a biscuit box.

By the time she was handed over to Freddy Smith in Framingham, Bluey was in a coma. Close to death, she took Freddy with her on a Magic Trip.

Louis had this notion of returning to England and us both buying a house together with the money I got from advance royalties on THE CARDBOARD COWGIRL.

Of course, I had other ideas. I had just finished Part 36 of my new novel. I had found a format that allowed me to write about anything and any place I liked. Admittedly, the travelling helped to give the book a bit of spice, but underneath it all, the meat of my writing was my imagination. I mean, it was all so far-fetched.

However, I knew that out there, out where the normal people go day-on-day, the imaginations of a million, no, ten million Britons were being trapped morn-till-night by social realism Louie loved to write. Social realism is everywhere. Even if the newspapers make up their stories, they try to make it sound real. If there's a play on telly, then no matter how absurd the plot, the director's got to make it seem real.

You've got to understand, there's this obsession amongst artists that makes them record and copy that which already exists. I mean, Aristotle had a lot to say about this sort of thing, but I won't go into that here. You see, the difference between an artist and an artisan is quite clear to me. An artist is a master of the imagination. An artisan is a master of artifice and technique.

It takes little imagination to sketch in words the movement of a clumsy man around a room. Who has not read such descriptions in the terse, dry novels of thriller suspense?

However, it is another matter all together to describe the spirit that fills the room that a clumsy man is snooping in. That man, the hero, call him what you may, is not the only feeling object in the room. As he opens a drawer or shuffles through secret papers, I can hear a drawer sigh "It's Rick the Dick", I can hear a paper moan "Piss off, you old detective fart."

You see, these writers who wring every bit of detail out of a running nose, fail to make any copy out of what the snot emerging from a nostril might have to say about it all. I mean, it all boils down to a lack of artistry.

As far as I can make out, lack of imagination is Louis's problem. He's hardly the most flamboyant individual. I mean, I know I've said we've split up, or at least I was going to get to that, but I suppose there is something to be said for people who have their two feet on the ground. I'm not sure what I'm trying to say, except that, even though Louis and I haven't been living together since we flew back from Bombay, I still see him.

I thought I had it in me to get it back together with Larry, but now I'm not so sure. I mean, if Louis had a bit more imagination, then maybe ...

You know, it really made me mad that he didn't even make any attempt to talk me out of going back to Larry.

God, I'll never understand men.

It's so frustrating. Every day I wonder if Louis is going to end up in my tea chest like all the other men in my life. Into my tea chest, that's where all my social realism goes. One day I'm going to sit down and make my tea chest talk like a society girl. It's full of tales about men. It might just seem to be a really dumb idea, but gosh, the stories it could tell. I was never a deb, but you would think from the way my tea chest talks about men that it was once a whore.

ZANE

I had this bloke once who was so

fantastic he could fly. You should have seen him in bed. He did it on a trapeze.

Yeah! A trapeze.

You can imagine my euphoria. He was weightless. All my old boys were such grinders. Meeting Zane was an absorbing experience. Know what I mean.

Well, there he was hovering above me like archangel Gabriel. I thought I was in heaven. We didn't even get the sheets dirty. When he moved in, my laundry bill halved.

The only drawback with doing it in space was that I had to have the whole ceiling of my boudoir reconstructed. When the handyman came he was speechless when the saw the juice stains on the light bulb and moulding. He gave us both such a look of smugness that he passed our telephone number on to his most sordid acquaintances.

You know the sort. Makes all his money from blackmailing housewives and milkmen. Anyway, when Zane came flying at him on his trapeze, the geezer's eyes nearly popped out of his head. Zane was naked. He looked so attractive.

I guess I didn't' realise what a great guy I had in Zane until that point. I had been taking him for the normal-head-on-the-pillow boring-once-a-day-once-a-night same position lover. But the more people I talked to about him, the more they told me they'd love to meet him, and asked me what time I usually went out. I came to understand that all the married girls who leer at guys in the bars would have wet *themselves to be introduced to Zane in a broom cupboard at a party.*

I felt sorry for them, there's not enough room in a broom cupboard to swing a cat never mind a trapeze. After all, that was Zane's speciality. The flying squirrel in the face is an unforgettable experience.

I would have liked to share him, but I couldn't get enough. He had me doing weigh training during the lulls.

I guess we were rather dull really. We'd start swinging and he would engulf me all the way. On one occasion my mum caught us hanging like this and commended Zane for obviously making me happy. She knew there would be a baby soon, but then again, that's what all mums think.

There was never any baby.

Zane and I lived happily in our swinging little flat which was our only steady base. We were once a cosy pair of birds.

When Chrissy and I flew out of Bombay for England I felt great. For the non-Asian, the greatest feeling experienced in Asia is the leaving of it. It doesn't matter if it's a flight from Tokyo, Bangkok, Kathmandu, or Delhi, as long as the wheels kiss the runway goodbye, and the ground recedes in a blur of memories.

> *Summertime oft green and wet,*
> *I can't remember yet.*
> *It's been two years since I've been here,*
> *It's been my one regret.*

I'm no poet like Chrissy. I think I said

that once before. I just can't take it
seriously like her.

> The sunshine of these foreign lands
> Has turned my skin to black,
> But little is it understood
> It's just a bloody tan.

See what I mean. Chrissy would never
write something like that. I just don't have
it. The talent. Is that what it takes? I don't
really know. I wrote it when we were
somewhere over Turkey. Chrissy just
laughed. She thought it was a fun piece. It
was so deflating. I had really tried to write
a serious poem. Chrissy made me feel even
worse when over Austria she wrote a poem.

TOO LATE TO CATCH THE SUN

> We wan and waste whale white Brits,
> we sit before our fires and freeze,
> our blotch red cheeks blue-vein cracked,
> our joints arthritic, stiff, and knocked,
> all wrack rheumatic, pinched, shagged,
> we huddle nursing heart-attacks.

Chrissy can hide behind words. I can't.
I'm just poor old Louis, poor bloody no-
hope unimaginative Louis. All I can tell you
about is what I did, or what Chrissy did, or
what we did, or what they did whoever they
are. I can never tell you about what might
have happened, or could have occurred, or
will one day come about. I've no
imagination. My feet are on the ground,
and they're there to stay. Chrissy's on a

completely different plane.

I mean, when we stepped off the plane at Heathrow, well, we were both on the same plain. It was all as clear as rain to me. Chrissy was going back to Larry.

And me?

I was going to go back North. Yeah, North. You know, that place where there are more dustbins than jobs. That's where I came from.

No, I was not going back to where little Loius Stewart started out life. No, I was never going back there. I mean, Newcastle, rotten stinking old Newcastle-upon-Tyne. It was my home.

Meanwhile I just couldn't keep up with Chrissy's literary ideas. I left.

LOLA

Magic trips don't usually have names. But this one did. She was called Lola and she came on nice and easy and put the mind at ease. Her world moved slow, but in wondrous ways that made Magic Trippers doubt whether such exquisiteness was real. She played soft and gentle to her voyagers, like a flute in the hands of a creative genius. Yet her music had a melancholic lilt that forced the purer Spirits to succumb to the Devils of Mischief. To explain would be to dispel the Magic of the Moment. But leave untold Lola's parting would be to leave off the reason of this digression.

Lola the Magic Trip ... was a bummer for Henrico, a room-head from sunny Acapulco who spent the autumns working in the apple-yards of Washington. Mad Joe Redhair, the beady-eyed Oregon homesteader on a business trip, had brought Lola Magic trip to the orchards and turned sibling Henrico on to her devastating charms.

Hec the Mex, a man unfamiliar with the moods of his own native peyote, fell down shivering in a fever in the orchard, convinced he was going to die. Mad Joe Redhair, fat and flush with dollars, told him he was just a little out of his head.

Henrico, permanently affected by Lola Magic Trip, vowed never to trust the word of another red-haired American again. He finished up the season in the orchards and went back to Acapulco to deal marijuana to the tourists.

I had lost Louie. The travelling had stopped and things were beginning to change. It was difficult to keep the momentum of my novel going.

After seeing a bit of the world, England seemed even more boring than ever.

But in reality I knew what the problem was. I missed Louis.

HENRICO's REVENGE

Tourists come in all shapes and sizes, but it is the Americans that the sharks like to take bites out of best of all.

Call it business acumen, or what you may, but there is little more pleasing in the daily dealings of a street-wise hustler than the outsmarting of a fat capitalist North American.

Admittedly, Mexicans themselves are North Americans, but there is no American in his right mind who will admit that. This establishes an impasse from the outset of any Ameri-Mex = Mex-Ameri relationship.

In Henrico's town of Acapulco, whoever has the most dollars has the most to lose. As Mexicans live on pesos and no real American wishes to soil his fingers on a Lopez or a Juarez. It is a one-way market of

Ameri supply = Mex demand.

Of course, this is a totally unfair way to look at this less than straightforward equation, especially when the Mexicans are in general nicer people than the Americans they have to deal with. But niceness has no place in the business world of

I want = Marijuana/Muchacha/Cerbeza

This was Henrico's line. In particular, it worked on freckle-faced West Coast redheads out to score some peyote. Henrico had his revenge on at least half a dozen of them before he mellowed out the effects of Lola Magic Trip.

There was no word from Louis. After I had picked up my tea chest from Alice and gone to stay with my brother in Somerset, I had heard nothing from him. He had gone north to Tyneside but he didn't write or phone or anything. I had decided not to go back to Larry who came to see me as soon as I got back. The past was the past and we both knew that we couldn't recapture the good times. It was strange that Larry wanted to stay on in England; I could never quite understand why he never went back to the States after we split up. But all I could think about was Louis.

Meanwhile, my writing was all shot to hell. I didn't know where I was going with my novel any more. I was getting off fiction and into politics. I was really unhappy.

CANE AND ABEL

Henrico's Revenge is symptomatic of the North-South, West-East split. Call it karma for lack of any other term.

Cause and effect?

It's the same old stone in the same old pond. Time after time, the same ripples are made. A bit like Northern Ireland ... you kill Jack ... I kill you ... Shaun kills me ... Billy me brother kills him ... and on and on and on. A never-ending future from an action committed at the beginning of time.

Cane and Abel?

And while this stuff goes on, karma comes down on everyone. The bills haven't been paid. The landlord's on your back for the rent. The schoolteacher's been on the phone about the kids. The boss balled you out. The car's broken down. Your granny's broke her leg. The washing machine's flooded the kitchen. The dog's eaten dinner. The budgie's died.

Karma comes down on everyone.

Still no word from Louis.
How I love him! How I miss him!
O Louis where are you?

KARMA

Karma brought baby Julie into the world. She was the direct result of her mother and father copulating.

After the conception came the ideal.
And then the reality.
It was all so beautiful, so simple, so natural. Julie was ten pounds, twelve ounces.
The father was ecstatic. The mother was a little tired, but feeling fine.

Louis had forsaken me. The pain got worse as the weeks went by. My brother Harry told me to chase after him.

"What's stopping you from going up to Newcastle?"

"I can't do that" I said.

"I think you're an ass, Chris. You should eat some of that pride of yours."

"It's not very palatable" I moaned.

"O for god's sake!" Harry bellowed. "You can't go on like this. You're flooding the house with tears."

I broke down and cried.

"Jesus! I've never seen anything like it" said Harry.

I cried even more.

And so it went on. The heartache

increased every day until eventually I was so ill I had to be confined to bed.

"Quite common" I heard the doctor say to Harry. "She'll probably die."

"Die?" quoth Harry.

"Fraid so. That's what usually happens in these cases."

"But it's only love-sickness?"

"And melancholia. The mind just gives up on the body."

"What's to be done, doctor?" Harry asked.

"The only effective cure is to find the cause."

"But we know the cause" said Harry.

"Then the cause will have to be brought here."

"But he lives in Newcastle!"

"He might live in Wangabanga for all I know, but usually they live just up the road. The only cure is to bring the fellow here."

The doctor left, and poor Harry took on the entire weight of my love affair with Louis.

SEPTIMUS

Julie had three sisters, April, May, and June.

All four were the joy of their parents until April, May, then June went off the tracks.

To be temporarily off the rails is no big deal, but to be off the line for good is a hard scrap-breaker reality for over-reactionary parents.

Julie was their pride and joy. She was their last and final flower before the arrival of their autumn years.

Then in a late bloom, mother produced three young boys ... Augustus, Septimus, and Octavius. They were products of their parent's love of history and imperialism that is part and parcel of growing old.

All three sons turned into little Mussolini's who stomped on one another on their way to ultimate supremacy. Augustus was the first to style himself 'El Duce', but it was Octavius who was first to call himself 'Caesar'. Septimus felt rather out of it as he could not think of an alternative name that rivaled the grandeur of his two brothers' choices.

Then one day, it came to him after he fell down a flight of steps and immediately became clairvoyant.

'Garibaldi'

"Garibaldi!" the others shouted in mockery "He was nothing but a lame old man who couldn't keep anything together."

Septimus, extremely hurt by the taunts of his two brothers, ran away from home. Before he departed, he quietly said goodbye to Julie who kissed him so passionately that he fell in love with her and vowed that one day he would return and rescue her from the tyranny of Augustus and Octavius.

From my window I could see the hens chasing the sparrows off the side lawn. Harry lived in a very large house in the Quantocks and it is there that I spent my most miserable hours. A few friends came and visited and tried to cheer me up but it was no use. I lay in bed reading Wordsworth as I felt he was the only poet who truly understood the nature of melancholy. I was not well versed in the Latin poets, not the Greek, so my despondency was shared mainly with Wordsworth. It was fitting that he had written his *Lyrical Ballads* on the hills behind Harry's house and I felt that if I were going to die, then it was fitting that it was in the bosom of the Quantocks.

I had learned from Harry that they had tried to trace Louis but that he had gone off to some hermitage in Scotland. There were so many hermitages in Scotland that they could not find out which one Louis had secluded himself in. But I knew. Louis had often talked about the place to me.

TYRANNY

Tyranny is a thing most Britons are familiar with when someone brings up the name of their first woman Prime Minister.

"Bloody fascist!" they scream in certain salient moods. "Fixed the hole in the economic bucket, but broke the handle off it while doing it."

Fine sentiments. It was no isolated opinion.

"Economic bucket?" a voice queried sceptically. "There were so many people out of work, there was no-one to carry it, never mind fill it."

Admittedly, there were a few rash

voices who viewed such wry affairs not as the product of tyranny, but one step removed from paradisiacal perfection.

"There are a thousand beautiful places in the world ... and five hundred of them are in England. Now you're lucky if you can find four hundred and ninety nine outside of the U.K. since we gave away Belize. There would have been even less if he had not beautified the Falklands."

Tyranny and imperialism go hand in hand. Anyone who vows to rescue anyone from tyranny under such a regime, can soon find themselves jobless, penniless, and on their way to jail.

Harry brought me a boiled egg, but it stuck in my throat and I nearly choked to death.

"This can't go on, Chris" he said as I cleared the tears from my eyes.

How many times had I heard him say that since I had fallen ill? He didn't realise that melancholy was a serious mental illness. After a while he thought that I was playing a silly game. One day he got me out of bed, put me in an invalid chair and wheeled me to the top of Cothelstone Hill.

"There" he said "Isn't that worth living for!"

"The view was fantastic, you could see right across Somerset to the edges of Dartmoor. Even more spectacular was the coast of Wales that was clearly visible across the other side of the Channel. It was beautiful.

"There" said Harry "I hope this shows

you that there is more to life than just one man."

He was right of course. But the longer I stared at the view, the more it reminded me of Darjeeling, of Hawaii, of Baja. I suddenly burst into tears.

Harry had to wheel me back to the house. I went into a sort of coma for a few days. I don't remember much. When I eventually came to, I mustered up enough strength to carry on with my novel.

PRISONS

Jail is where I started my story, so why go back there. Who wants to be cooped up in a cell when the whole beautiful world is spinning round and round. We all live in our own prisons anyway, so who needs to hear about someone else's.

Harry felt so awful about what he had done to me, he started going to church. He felt that prayer was the only thing that was going to save me.

Deep down I couldn't help laughing, but it hurt so much I didn't laugh for long. Unknown to me, Harry had hired a detective to find Louis, and sure enough, he tracked him down at the Buddhist retreat in Eskdalemuir. I knew that Louis had been there all along, for after his flying trip round India with Mat Gandhi, Louis had told me about how he had once spent time at Eskdalemuir. It was the only place that Louis had to hide out in Britain. I could hide at Harry's, but Louis's had nowhere like that. His family were poor, his mum and dad lived in a council house. And because Louis came from the North, all his friends were poor too.

It is sad really. The only escape for a Northerner like Louis is institutional. There are no real old ramshackle homes like Harry's. Not for Louis. Not for someone who comes from a council home.

Lying in bed at Harry's, I began to feel this great guilt well up inside me. I had lost my ability to speak. Great dark clouds went round and round in my head. My only link with the world was my writing.

HELEN HONEYCUTT

Helen Honeycutt's prison was Hillbrow, Johannesburg.

Talking of tyranny, Helen was a right ball-buster. She loved taking shy black-boys to Swaziland to milk them dry. She'd talk the poor kaffir's ear off all evening then expect the poor mealie-muncher to crawl to her sexual demands.

Helen as she was ... she was an insult to pigs. She was beneath comparison with earth's creatures. She was pure Anglo-Aryan. Two hundred and fifty pounds? And a sight to see squashed into a Volkswagen 'beetle'.

How her lover boys put up with such a colossal task was to take her lying down. Invariably, the very expanse of her flesh immediately drained them.

Helen worked for the South African immigration office. She had an endless supply of 'wrong-doing' kaffirs willing to kiss their way out of transportation and labour camp. Every weekend she selected an African and took him to Swazi where he was expected to satisfy her. If the dumb-dog didn't have the brains to run out on her and cross the border into Mozambique, she'd bring him back to Joburg and have him transported off to work in the fields of a Bantustan.

Helen was a good South African. That's why she and her country were fucked.

I was down to ninety-nine pounds. They got me out of bed one day and weighed me. The doctor wanted to know if they had found the cause of my weight loss.

"Yeah" said Harry "He's gone all religious. He's become a monk."

"Then there's no hope" said the doctor.

I saw a huge grey cloud. The window was open, and as Harry and the doctor discussed the hopelessness of my condition, the cloud hovered above the house.

I knew.

"Louis!" I cried, "You've come for me." I tried to get out of bed. I had to go to the window.

"My god!" despaired Harry and the doctor as they caught hold of me.

"She's insane, doctor."

I knew Louis was waiting for me.

"She'll have to go into care" said the doctor.

"No, no, I can't allow that" answered Harry.

"You must get the monk!" said the

doctor.

"Louis ... Louis" I whispered.
"Well?" asked the doctor.
Harry nodded.
I faded into a dream.

DROOPING FUCHSIA

Drooping Fuchsia, a Tokyo geisha girl, was always fucked on the local liquor. Between sushi dishes she'd always fuddle her brain with a potent saki beverage. She wasn't meant to drink on the job, but her customers would coax her to indulge in their celebratory habits ... particularly the unwashed foreigners ignorant of Japanese protocol.

But Fujiyama ... Drooping Fuchsia could handle it. The money was good, and the work was light when compared with the harsh peasant life of the mountains. Tokyo was no garden, but at least the grass was greener. Tokyo was thin on fresh air, but at least that was preferable to too much.

Yes ... Drooping Fuchsia got fucked and fuddled a lot. On her days off she liked nothing better than frequenting the tea gardens to admire the cascades of flowers which made Japan so beautiful.

I was down to seventy-nine pounds when Harry departed. He was gone for a few days and had left one of these awful Conservative Party women to look after me. Her name was Agnes, and she might as well have been called Agony the way she treated me. Apart from her name, everything else about her is a haze.

She was cruel.

The first lunchtime, Agony forced me to eat a three-course meal. I had barely eaten a thing for months, the odd sip of soup, the occasional nibble of bread. I could no longer eat eggs since I had nearly choked on the one Harry had brought me that time.

What I lived on was my love for Louis.

Agony thought I was nuts. It was all over face. She had never been in love in her life. Or so I thought until I found out that she had once been engaged to a vicar's son.

So if nothing else, we had one thing in common. Both of us had experience of religious men. I think the main difference though was that I had met my man before be had become religious. Agony's man had gone the other way. He had been all set to take the cloth like his father when he had developed this love of gambling, and drinking. And well, before you know it, one thing leads to another. Other women. Debt. Marxism. In the end he went off to help the Sandanistas fight the Contras in Nicaragua.

She hated me.

I was scribbling out Part 46 of novel when she suddenly grabbed it and began to read it. Fortunately enough, 46 was very inoffensive.

"What's this? Your writin' then?" she asked in a hiss.

"It's the history of..."

"This is no history" she snapped. "Who's this Pink Fuchsia?"

"She's one of life's heroines."

"It's rubbish. You wouldn't find some'it like this in Women's Own!"

She had no idea how happy she made me feel when she said that.

"I think writin' this sort of rubbish is makin' you ill," she said. "So while I'm lookin' after you, they' be no more of this." She crumpled up my writing and ate it.

I could have murdered her. She looked so smug, you could have played Jingle Bells on her teeth. The next thing she did was to nail up the window.

"We don't want you gettin' any silly ideas, do we now?" she said waving the hammer in my face. She was absolutely nuts. I thought she was going to nail shut the bedroom door as well, but instead she force fed me three bananas, three apples, and a bag of grapes.

"We want you better, don't we?" she laughed. I knew that before long she would be sexually assaulting me. Her hand touched my breast.

"Now, you hav' a good nap, dear, and I' be back up this evenin' with your supper."

The horror departed.

I lay for an hour in a fear. I was so afraid that I didn't even think of Louis once. I slumbered, then awoke, slumbered, and then awoke. I pulled out a pen and some paper I had hidden under my pillow, and began once again on Part 46.

PINK FUCHSIA

Drooping's sister, Pink Fuchsia, was a different type of girl. She worked for

Japanese Airlines as a hostess, and made sure that most of the first class passengers got fuddled on Johnny Walker during the flight. Of course, it was hardly the same Johnny Walker that had gone ashore at Diego Garcia, by seemingly, it tasted pretty much the same to the commander who had taken a week's leave to go and climb Fujiyama.

Pink, on the other hand, was about to catch a few days off in Perth, Australia, but when the plane got hi-jacked over the South China Sea, they were all suddenly on their way to an unknown destination.

Naturally, Pink was very upset that her holiday arrangements would have to be rescheduled, and in no uncertain terms, she gave one of the three hijackers a good mouthful of Japanese dialect.

Almost as naturally, the hijacker told her to shut up. It was his assumption that Pink had gone into a hysterical fit in the face of their armed take over of the plane.

In conceit, the hijacker grabbed Pink around the waist, and kissed her.

Outraged, Pink high-balled the Jack so hard he dropped his weapon. In a flash, the commander had palmed the weapon and beaten the hijacker over the head with it.

Half an hour later, all three hijackers were securely bound in the baggage section. The plane was once more on course for Perth.

That night, the commander took Pink out for dinner aboard a NATO sub.

Evening came. I could hear the dogs

howling because they hadn't been fed. The moon was over Dead Woman's Ditch. Shafts of eerie light flooded through the cracks in the nailed up window.

Then I heard Agnes's footsteps. She was climbing the stairs. Every step creaked. There was the sound of shuffling. Things were going bump in the night. I was terrified.

The bedroom door opened. A flood of light fell across my bed. Agnes stood silhouetted in the doorway.

"I'v brought you som' supper, dear" she hissed.

I cowered under the bedclothes.

"Com' along, dear" she said pulling back the bed sheets "I'v a Conservative Party meetin' to go to!"

I could feel her wash-red hands on my legs. She'd been scrubbing the floors.

"I'v got to giv' you a bed bath afore you can hav' your supper."

I was terrified.

A wet cold cloth fell on my stomach.

"Now, ain't that nice then?" she said as the cloth travelled down in between my legs. "Nothin' like a nice bed bath" she said as her fingers began forcing open my vagina. "I ain't got much time now" she said "but I be back after the meetin'."

The bed bath stopped.

"Your supper be gettin' cold, girl" she laughed.

She replaced the bedclothes and smoothed out the bedspread.

"Here it be" she said. "Some nice fresh chicken. Now that you don't eat eggs, then, no point in havin' hens, is there?"

She knew I was a vegetarian.

"I'll leave you be, then" she said. "My meetin', you see. But I be back to give you some cocoa."

She laughed such an evil laugh the whole house shook.

"I be back!

THE GREAT DIVIDE

Eventually the Commander got to come home on his NATO sub. England was sighing under the weight of policemen's Billy clubs, but only in the cities, and only in the West and North.

At a Gentleman's Dinner, the Southerners headed by the Commander were trying to tell Colonel Jock Wilson that the North began at Watford Gap. Jock just laughed at the lot of them.

"You silly wee Sassenach" he pitied them. "You haven't a canny clue aboot a bloody thing, pals!" Jock was very demonstrative. "You see, you sozzled nancies, the North, man..."

"Come on, Jock" a Navy officer corrected him "Get your syntax … you know?"

He was very vague. Jock just looked at him with a blank Highland stare as if the Englishman was nothing more important than a sprig of heather in a Glasgow garden.

"Men ... I shall never appeal to you" said Jock. "Consequently, you shall never sentence me to your notions of how I

should be. We Northerners, and when I say Northerners, I mean, real Northerners, anyone north of Inverness..."

"Ha, ha, ha!" the Southerners laughed.

"And what's the matter with you, nasty sassies?" Jock bellowed "Can't you accept the truth like men!"

Just then Dubliner Niall O'Rourke, who had been biting his tongue, plunged into the fray.

"What about us Westerners then?"

"Westerners?" a Commander quizzed.

"You know ... " another Southerner interceded "People who live west of Windsor."

"O them" another Home Counties gentlemen said, "Not many of them, are there? Hardly a force of national importance."

"What about the East?" a rather perplexed French guest inquired.

"Essex, you mean" a Southern gentleman corrected him. There were certainly a lot of Southern gentlemen at the dinner. "That is where one lives if one cannot afford a house in the South."

"I do not understand" the Frenchman said.

"Don't you fret, Pierre" Jock Wilson interrupted. "It's all baloney!"

"But what is this South they speak of?" Pierre asked.

"It is where you get your passport stamped" a Southerner answered him.

"The North is where you go with it" the Commander said.

"The West is where your breakfast

bacon and butter comes from" a third said to the Frenchman.

"The East ... I wouldn't bother with it" the Navy officer said. "I'd stay in the South if I were you."

"But France is South of here. This is north to me, n'est pas?" Pierre smiled.

"Where is France?" a Southerner asked.

"Where is Scotland?" another laughed.

"Or Ireland for that matter?" another added. All the Southerner's laughed and chuckled to one another.

"Never were very good at geography, these Londoners" Jock said to Francis and Pierre "Yet they'll drink our whiskey, wine, and water. The South is the national plughole. We pour it out, they drain it away."

All the Southerners fell silent. Someone dropped his upper-lip and it sounded like thunder.

"Gentlemen" Colonel Jock Wilson continued "Let us toast one another as Europeans!"

"Here Here!" the chorus resounded around the room. "To Europe!"

They raised their glasses.

"Where's Europe?" a Southerner whispered to the Commander.

"Everywhere but in the South" the Commander whispered back.

I was trapped in the West Country. I was expecting Agnes back from the Conservative party meeting any moment.

The house was empty, and the moon was going down. I lay in the dark imagining

Agnes's footsteps on the stairway. I had no idea what had happened to Harry. Perhaps Agnes had done him in.

I heard the front door opening.

THE HITCHHIKER

After the dinner party, Jock Wilson drove blind sober back to his country home. On the way he picked up a young man. Penniless and dressed like a monk, the young man was gaunt and serious.

"Yer no a Southerner, are ye?" Jock asked him in curiosity.

"No, I'm from Newcastle" the young man replied politely.

They didn't say much else to one another. When Jock dropped the man off at an M5 slipway, he said

"Ye must be cauld! Here take this!" He thrust a ten pound note into the man's hand and said "Aw the best, son. And here, you'll need this an'aw." He threw him a plastic raincoat.

The young man watched him drive off.

The traffic droned on by into the English night. The Geordie donned the raincoat and stood shivering in the autumn dark.

He had a hundred miles to go.

I heard the front door closing. I heard the sound of water dripping on the carpet!

It was Agnes!!

The meeting was over and now she came for me.

"It be me" she whispered "It be me."

I heard her footsteps on the stairs.

"It be me!" she said "It be me with your cocoa!

JOURNEY'S END

The monk was only a mile away from his destination.

He asked the way at the local inn, and the landlord pointed him up a long dark lane.

"Broomfield Hall be that way" he shivered. "You be alone?" he asked

"Aye" said the monk.

"Well, god be with you" the landlord said.

"He is" replied the monk.

The monk travelled up the long dark lane towards the Hall. There was something sure and steady in his gait that was purposeful. He passed under the oak known as Enmore Gibbet, but his aura silenced all the attending spirits. They were afraid of this holy man, this strange monk. Where had he come from? Why was he there?

An owl screeched in a beech tree. The monk creaked open the rusty gate at the entrance to the drive. Suddenly the Hall grounds were lit up with a blinding white light.

The monk smiled. He had reached his journey's end. Ahead lay the house. Above him the sky was aglow. He could hear singing, sweet singing.

In a few moments he would enter into eternal happiness.

"I've brought you your cocoa, dear"

hissed Agnes. "I had a lovely meetin' an' that. We planned the autumn fair. It was ever so nice. I would hav' stayed longer but I had be back to giv' you your cocoa."

Agnes pulled back the bedclothes.

"Now there be a good girl. I ne'er did finish your body bath."

I lay there. I knew that this was the end.

"My, you'v' such lov'ly skin, dear."

She ran her hands all over my body.

My heart was broken.

She kissed me.

I died.

THE END

Louis had come.

He carried me down the stairs and out of the house. There was an angel waiting.

I looked at Louis.

"You may take one thing from this earth with you" the angel said.

"One thing?" I asked

"He has chosen you" said the angel. "Now, before we depart, you may choose whatever you wish."

I thought. But I had already decided.

"My tea chest" I whispered.

"So be it. Are you ready?" the angel asked.

Louis and I looked at one another. We knew.

We were on our way to heaven.

"Then let us go," said the angel with a smile.

He carried us up into the star-lit night,

and as we travelled through joy and bliss, I knew I finally been released from my prison where no light entered and no sound exited. I was no longer alone. I heard birds, and I could see the wonders of the universe. I had no past; there was only a future. Where we were going was full of light. There, up there I would be able to write in peace for time immortal.

And my salvation? It is no secret. It is so within me that I feel the whole world must know. I know people will listen. These heavens are not silent; each star is a day of time.

My mind is now at one with my body. I have repented my past. I am warm and well fed. I know that I will never die.

I have Louis.

And I have my tea chest.

ROBBIE MOFFAT

The author was born and schooled in Glasgow. He took a degree in English language and Literature at Newcastle University. He began writing when he was seventeen and has a had a career as a poet, novelist, playwright and screenwriter. He is best known for his feature film work in which he is also a director and producer.

His prose writing as been overshadowed by this. He wrote his first novel when he was twenty two and continued to write novels for the next twenty years. None of them were published.

The rediscovery of his prose work has lead to a recent spate of publications that has lead to a resurgence of interest in his prose writing.